AI

All my life I've been dreaming up stories. My mum said when I was little I used to make all the My Little Pony figurines talk to each other and even fall in love. Later, it was Barbie and Ken. In my teens, I played matchmaker with my friends at school. When I wasn't creating imaginary scenarios, I had my nose stuck in books, reading across genres and there was one thing I loved more than the escapism—the fact a story could touch me so deeply, like I was experiencing everything along with my characters. I knew from early on this was something I wanted to do for others.

Fast forward a few years and the dream almost got lost in real life, but I still couldn't shake it completely. Now I write sizzling romance with the hope of making my readers' hearts race as if they are falling in love for the first time.

# What's a Girl to Do?

## AIMÉE DUFFY

Harper*Impulse* an imprint of
HarperCollins*Publishers* Ltd
77–85 Fulham Palace Road
Hammersmith, London W6 8JB

www.harpercollins.co.uk

A Paperback Original 2014

First published in Great Britain in ebook format by Harper*Impulse* 2013

A catalogue record for this book
is available from the British Library

ISBN: 978-0-00-755969-5

Automatically produced by Atomik ePublisher from Easypress

*To Chelle, Amalie, Cat/Jo, Amy, Mel and the Dashing ladies. I really appreciate having you all, especially when I'm whining.*

# Chapter One

*Tonight's a tequila night, screw the lime mixer.*

Shey Lopez grinned at Georgia's email to her and their other roommate, Eloisa. No doubt about it, the week had dragged and she was up for something stronger than their usual pitcher of frozen margaritas.

She hit *reply to all* and got typing.

*I'm in.*

Jude Graham chose that second to clear his throat at the door to her office. She fought back a scowl at her boss and hit CTRL & E without glancing at the screen. The high-maintenance bitch looked flustered, which was ironic since he'd barely lifted a finger all week. His whole *me editor, you do what I tell you* attitude got on her nerves. If *Storm* wasn't the best fashion magazine in New York, she'd be out of there faster than Jude could buff his fingernails. And, going by the way that they shined, he was a pro.

'What can I do for you, Jude?' Surely he could tell the saccharine tone of her voice was false. Then again, being false was one of Jude's many talents.

'I need those proofs for the Gianni article by the end of the day.'

Shey's smile slipped. He'd given her the paperwork less than an hour ago and it was already way past three. The guy was a nightmare, too busy wrapped up in another argument with his

1

husband to care about his job. She couldn't wait for the day she cranked up enough experience to leapfrog over his ass and be the editor, not the assistant.

'There's only two hours left and I have other work to do,' she said, sounding calm, even though her heart rate increased with trepidation. Still, she was playing over all the insults she could think of in her mind.

He scowled, or tried to. The botox didn't leave much room for changes in his expression. 'There's more than one smart-assed girl in this building who would kill for your position. If the article isn't on my desk at five, you can kiss your job goodbye.'

With that and more flourish than a prom queen, he left. Shey was tempted to launch her stapler at the empty doorway, but resisted. Everything good in life came with a price, or so she told herself. Her dream job should have a downside, it was only the natural balance of things. That little bitch Jude was what she had to suffer to get to the top, and she would suffer him and do it with a smile.

Closing her eyes, she took a calming breath. And then another. Her yoga instructor would be proud.

With her head cleared, she got her focus back in the game. Jude would have his article on the desk by four forty-five. She could do this. And later, when her head was frazzled and her fingers ached, she'd go out with her girls and drink the well dry.

Opening a new email, she sent another message to Georgia and Eloisa.

*The bitch is at it again. Make mine doubles.*

After hitting *send*, she got to work.

\*\*\*

With half an hour to spare, Shey was relieved her speedy fingers and dedication meant she'd get to see Jude's jaw drop. Three

2

read-throughs later and the article was as polished as she could make it, but she wasn't kidding herself that it would be enough. Little bitch, or LB as most of the office staff called him, was pernickety and thorough. One mistake or missing word and he'd come down on her so hard that some would think she'd made an attempt on his husband's life.

Tapping the pointed toes of her Prada stilettos, Shey waited for the article to print. When it was done she aligned the pages, stapled the top corner, and made a beeline for Jude's office.

*Storm* was exactly what she had expected when she'd landed the internship over a year ago. All white plastic with brightly colored furniture and art. Bitches around every corner waiting to stab you in the back to get on their editor's good sides. And the jackpot: free backstage passes to fashion shows, exclusive clubs, and parties. God, she loved it. She really did. But she suspected the cattiness was rubbing off on her. When she'd started the internship she'd been quiet, too scared to say boo to anyone. She learned quickly that if she didn't stand up for herself and grow a backbone, she'd be crushed like a bug.

Rounding the corner she spied what her friends would call 'a suit' talking to the receptionist, Mandy. Shey slowed her steps, taking him in from side profile. That body was built, in a Brad Pitt kind of way, with much better arm definition. Dark-chestnut hair grew long enough to cling on to and he had skin as dark as her own, which meant he was either half-Latina like her or paid a few visits a week to the tanning booth.

Either way, hot as sin.

When he turned and she met his hazel gaze, her skin warmed like it was on fire. The white cotton shift dress she'd donned for work suddenly felt as thick as a quilt and she had trouble getting air into her lungs. Christ, the guy must've been throwing some kind of freaky pheromones her way. Either that or it had been way too long since she'd had a date.

His gaze roved over her body from her head to the scarlet Prada's

3

and he didn't make any effort to hide his scrutiny. He was a ten, at least. And thank you God! There was no mistaking he liked what he saw, if his wink was anything to go by. Most guys who came for a meeting at *Storm* were gay. This hottie either swung both ways or he was all about the ladies. Shey didn't really care which, as long as she was on the list of things that made him burn.

Pulling her shoulders back, she added a sashay to her hips as she approached him. There was plenty of time to get the paperwork to Jude and, if she could find out something about Mr. Tall, Dark, and Built, she didn't mind being a little late. After all, who else would he find to put up with his bullshit? She'd been the only intern who got promoted to assistant editor last year. The others would crack within a week.

She did a little looking of her own as she approached, giving him points for the navy tailored suit, deducting a few for not wearing a tie. Ties were sexy. She could pull a guy over for a kiss with it, or slide it off then wrap it around his eyes while she led him to the bedroom. More points for rockin' the open collar on the white silk shirt, especially since the skin underneath was smooth and bronzed.

Determined to play it cool, Shey headed to the reception instead of approaching the guy.

'You hitting the town with us tonight?' Shey asked. Mandy was one of the few in the office that Shey could actually stand. Her housemates liked Mandy too.

Mandy bit her cherry-glossed lip. 'Club Zero?' Shey nodded. 'I can't. Graham wants me to watch the game with him tonight. He says doing more stuff together will bring us closer.'

Shey tried not to screw up her face and failed. 'Watching the game, seriously? Like the Yankies are going to make up for months of no dates or attention?' She pitied poor Mandy and wished she had the balls to ditch that loser. She was gorgeous, all busty and blonde, and that guy treated her like an afterthought.

A husky laugh made her turn.

4

'I suppose you agree with her idiot boyfriend?' Shey asked the stranger.

His lips twisted up at the corners and a sultry look darkened his eyes. 'Hell no. I can think of better ways to entertain a lady.'

Her heart rate went crazy.

Mandy gasped, but was saved by the phone ringing. Shey didn't have the same time to compose herself. She was lost in his gaze and that fiery burn scorching through her body. For the first time since she could remember, Shey couldn't find her tongue. Those damn eyes messed with her head and she couldn't break free from their spell if she tried.

He stepped closer and the burn intensified. She was so hot she wanted to rip the dress off and stand in front of an open freezer to cool down. Up close she could see a dark five o'clock shadow on his sculpted jaw. His throat was thick, just like his shoulders. The slightly crooked nose suggested he'd had it broken at some point in his life, but it didn't deter from his harsh beauty. Shey was awestruck, and so turned on she thought she might come just from looking at him.

'What's your name, gorgeous?' he asked.

The disinterest on his face made it seem like he was flirting out of habit rather than because he wanted to. Even still, there seemed to be a magnetic force between them, crackling in the air and sparking. Those eyes of his had darkened, contradicting his Mr. Cool Man front. No way was Shey going to make this easy for him.

'Seriously? That the best line you've got?' She forced a laugh, but it came out husky, damn it. 'Next you'll call my dad a thief for stealing the stars and putting them in my eyes.'

His brows shot up, but he composed himself in a heartbeat. With a smile, he leaned forward and brushed a kiss over her cheekbone. The spicy smell of him invaded her senses and her skin sizzled with the contact. Her body went hyperactive. Hands trembling, knees weakening and oh yeah, soaked right through her lacy thong. She had to get away from him before she did something crazy, like beg for those soft lips to touch her again.

'Sweetheart, with you I don't need any lines.'

Anger boiled through her veins, loosening his hold on her body. She didn't even know his name and he had her salivating, for Christ's sake. He was a cocky bastard, so sure he had her right where he wanted her, and the worst thing? He was absolutely right. Next time those lips touched her skin she'd be putty in his long-fingered hands.

'It'll take more than arrogance to win me over.' Shey left the *asshole* unspoken. 'I have somewhere to be.' Without waiting for Mandy to get off the phone or for Mr. Cool to reply, she left reception.

His voice trailed behind her. 'I'll see you soon, gorgeous.'

*Yeah, big shot. In your dreams.*

\*\*\*

'Here's to Friday nights. Where would we be without them?' Georgia held up her shot of tequila.

From their table on the upper level of Club Zero, they had a bird's-eye view of the club below. Dark purple and chrome was the theme, and the whole place was surrounded by mirrored walls.

Shey clinked her shot against Georgia's and Eloisa joined in.

She was the first to get the glass to her lips and swallow in one go. The burn in her throat was bliss after a day like today. Even though she got the article in early, Jude had acted like, well, a bitch and made her redo three paragraphs. Surprise, surprise. And she wasn't even thinking about Mr. Cool.

It was almost nine and half the men in the club had already picked out the women they were going to dance with or take home. The rest were the ones other women had ditched for a reason. A quick glance around was all Shey and her roomies needed to find out why. Stragglers, Michelin Men, and the drooling desperados lurked in the shadows, waiting for the women to down a bit too much hard stuff.

There weren't thick enough beer goggles in the world.

Shey turned away with a sigh. It didn't matter who was left, she didn't do one-night stands. She liked to have a connection with the men she got involved with. Going home with a guy or vice versa was dangerous in more ways than one.

'We need to stop coming here after eight.' The earlier they arrived, the better chance they had of grabbing a table downstairs the perfect distance between the dance floor and the bar. Not to mention finding a guy or two who actually wanted to talk, not drool.

'You'd rather spend the night on EHarmony?' Eloisa asked with distaste and flicked her auburn curls over her shoulder. 'There are more psychos on the net. At least here you can see the ugly coming.'

'Or the desperate,' Georgia added.

'I don't think any of us will find what we're looking for in a bar,' Shey said.

'Speak for yourself.' Eloisa downed another shot. With watery eyes, she glanced at Shey. 'You're the only one uptight about dating.'

Her mouth dropped open. 'I'm not uptight, just careful.'

Georgia rolled her eyes. 'Come on, you've never even had a fling.'

'That's hardly a national disaster.'

Eloisa chimed in. 'It could be. Maybe the world needs Shey Lopez to do one wild thing.'

Shey shook her head. 'I've done wild things.'

'Yeah right.' Georgia picked up her glass. 'Splurging on a pair of shoes you can't afford is the craziest thing you've done.'

Being teased by her friends never usually bothered her, and it didn't this time either. If she took the bait it was sure to get worse. But she'd come out tonight for more in the way of fun, and damn if she wasn't going home until her feet throbbed and she'd had a good work out on the dance floor.

'Let's dance girls,' she said.

7

They finished the last of the tequila and headed down to the main level. Club Zero was no back-street club or for the lower class. The cover price to get in was her weekly indulgence, and the drinks all had a few extra dollars added to the price. But the best bit? No trash. It was the high end of sophistication in Manhattan and they could dance without worrying about getting spills all over their new stilettos.

Finding an open area near the bar, they tucked their clutch bags under their arms and got busy. By the third song, Shey was feeling more relaxed, her body loosening and the stress of the day disappearing. It was weird that she found the atmosphere in the club calming, considering all the strobe lights and neon, but burning up a good sweat swinging her hips was her favorite form of exercise. Probably had something to do with the tequila too.

Eloisa came close and pressed her body against Shey's. A typical move for her if there was a guy who caught her interest, so Shey went with it and grabbed her hips. Georgia was a few feet away, dancing with her eyes closed in that self-possessed way of hers, giving herself up to the beat of the music.

After a moment Shey realized Eloisa wasn't giving anyone the eye. Instead she leaned close and shouted in Shey's ear, 'don't look now, but there's a gorgeous suit at the bar checking you out.'

Nodding to let Eloisa know she got the message, Shey changed the position of their bodies until their satin-clad rears ground together as they danced. Shey missed a grind and almost fell backward when she saw who was staring, but she got back with the program quickly. Holy hell, Mr. Cool was here—in a different suit—and he was staring at her from beneath hooded lids.

With one arm propped on the bar and a tumbler containing dark liquid in his other hand, he looked *sexier* than sin. Then his earlier words came back and even though the heat still sizzled between them, Shey forced herself to turn away. The guy had an ego to rival Hugh Hefner's and could probably get a woman into his bed tonight with a click of his fingers. His bored tone, the disinterest in his expression, and his cocky remark about not needing a line meant he was not for her.

She liked a guy to make a little more effort than that before she decided whether or not she wanted to fall into bed with him.

Studiously ignoring him, she continued to shake what her mama gave her—though her mom would be horrified to see the size of Shey's hips. Felicity Lopez was on the curvy side for a supermodel but weighed a good twenty pounds less than Shey. No way was Shey going to live on rabbit feed for the rest of her life. Food, like life, was there to enjoy.

Eloisa called a time-out and headed back to the table with Georgia since it was Shey's round, and probably because they thought Shey was interested in Mr. Cool. She tried to act casual and crossed to the opposite end of the mahogany bar to avoid him. After placing the order for an army of shots, the bartender got to work.

'If I said these were on me, would you think that's another line?' Mr. Cool was standing right next to her and she had to take a deep breath to orientate herself.

That was the wrong thing to do. He'd switched the spicy after-shave for something musky and that had an even stronger effect on her hormones. Eau de Pheromone, maybe? She hoped it was expensive so all the creeps in the city didn't catch on.

Shey turned to him and squared her shoulders. 'I'd say I'm perfectly capable of buying my own drinks.' She fought the urge to thank him for the offer, especially when she saw the wry smile.

'How about we start again? I'm Calvin.' He extended his hand.

Placing her hand in his, she shivered at the electric contact. It woke up her insides like she'd swallowed a couple of hormone pills. His head bowed over her hand, but he never took his attention off her face. Her breath caught as his lips brushed her knuckles and she had to jerk her hand back.

The flash fire that burned over her skin was epic and worse, Shey wanted him to kiss her again. Crazy. Even though he seemed to be trying politeness on for size, he had this confidence that said he knew she'd end up naked on his bed, and though her body went wild with the idea, *no thanks.* Shey was the result of her mom's stupidity. Felicity had fallen for a charmer, and all it had done was stall her mother's career.

Quickest way to cut off his interest would be to lie through her teeth. 'Sorry, I have—'

'Shey, fibs are unattractive. I know you're single.' He stepped closer, too close, and her heart kicked off on a mamba.

'How do you know my name?'

And why did the sound of it rolling off his tongue get her even hotter?

Calvin smiled, showing every one of those flawless white teeth, and she was dazzled. Christ. She needed to pull it together, fast.

'Your friend Mandy and I spoke.'

Shey frowned. She was going to kill Mandy.

'A woman like you shouldn't be single. Unless you're the kind of woman who likes variety.'

'Another line?' She tried to hold the scowl, and failed. The way he said *variety* had her thinking about all the different things he'd do to her body. She had a feeling he'd take her higher than any man ever had, and that was based on her own reaction to him, not to mention that arrogant confidence which pissed her off and got her hot all at the same time.

'I told you earlier Shey, I don't need them.'

Saved by the shots. The bartender placed down a tray and, even though she'd ordered three for each of them, it didn't seem like enough. Hell, jumping into an ice bath didn't seem like enough to calm her down. She paid the guy and told him to keep the change. Before she managed to scamper away with the tray, Calvin spoke.

'I'll see you soon, Shey.'

She frowned at him, thinking that wasn't going to happen. 'You know, there's a club full of women here tonight who I'm sure would be more than happy to give you what you want.'

10

'What is it you think I want?'

Those eyes, all dark and intense, scrambled her thoughts. 'An easy lay.' The second the words left her lips, her face heated.

Calvin raised a dark brow. 'Where's the fun in that?'

She sent a message to her feet to get them to move, but they ignored her. She was trapped again, her body wanting what she wouldn't let it have and now she could see it in his expression. He was thriving on the challenge she'd presented him, instead of giving her a half-assed come-on like earlier.

But it didn't matter. When they met he'd hit on her in under three seconds, without even knowing her name, and those kind of guys didn't do fancy dates. They wanted women in their beds and if they had to work a little to make it happen, that was fine with them. She wasn't going to join the notches on his bedpost.

'You're wasting your breath with me.' This time when she turned to leave with the tray of much-needed tequila, her feet obeyed.

Calvin got the last word. Again. 'I always get what I want.'

# Chapter Two

Unease twisted Shey's empty stomach as she followed Mandy up the stairs on Monday afternoon. Why Marco, the big-dog editor and chief, would want his receptionist and an assistant editor to check out the upper floor was beyond her. She went anyway, clutching her purse tightly to her side. The sooner they got this over with and she could scoot to the deli across the street, the better. She was starved.

Mandy opened the door to the twelfth floor, and Shey's breath caught in her throat. Mr. Cool—Calvin—stood in the entrance lobby next to a table draped with a thick white cloth. A bottle of Merlot was open, two glasses poured and two candles lit, but she didn't notice what was on the plates. She couldn't take her eyes off of his.

'That will be all, Mandy.' His voice, gentle yet commanding, shivered through her.

Mandy scurried back to the stairwell just as Shey's shock cleared. She reached out and blocked the doorway with her arm.

'What the hell's going on here?' she asked them both, though it was pretty obvious. She'd been set up. The *you will not talk about me to strangers again* speech she'd given Mandy earlier had clearly gone in one ear and out the other.

'Shey, I hoped you would join me for lunch.' There was no

12

demand in his tone now, only charm, and she didn't trust it one bit.

'I think it's romantic.' Mandy let out a dreamy sigh and Shey rolled her eyes.

She couldn't deny the gesture was sweet, in its own way. She wanted a guy to make the effort for her, and Calvin had brought that in spades. Didn't mean she appreciated the sneaky way he got her there. Still, she gave him points for his smarts. There was no way she'd have come if she knew what was going on.

The effort alone deserved a gentle let-down, since her rejection on Friday night hadn't gotten through that beautiful head of his.

'Fine. I'll stay, but only because I'm starving.' And were those chocolate truffles? Yeah, she'd stay for dessert before she put her foot down.

Mandy winked, then she was off down the stairs with a clatter of heels hitting concrete. Wisely, Calvin didn't smirk, only pulled a chair out for her. She slid in, breathing through her mouth in case he was throwing out the bottled pheromones again.

He disappeared behind her and then she heard the click of the door closing. She whirled the top half of her body around to face him, a skitter of unease dancing down her spine. 'What are you doing?'

Part of her wondered if this was a bad idea. She was alone with a man who drove her body crazy, a man she barely knew. He could be a rapist or a murderer. But if he was either of those things, getting Mandy to bring her up here would blow his cover, wouldn't it? Mandy would know the last person Shey was with, and there was CCTV all over the building.

Calvin left the key in the lock and sauntered back to her with a manly gait that drew her gaze down his body to take in every inch of that tailored suit. Shit, even his walk was sexy. The corner of his mouth pulled up and her heart stuttered.

'I want to make sure no one interrupts us.'

She watched as he sat across from her at the table, wondering if what he said was true.

'I'm not going to hurt you, Shey. You don't need to be afraid of me,' Calvin said seriously.

Stupidly, she believed him. But he meant physically, not emotionally, and to her the latter was all that counted. 'Why lock the door? It's not as if anyone will come up here.'

One eyebrow rose as he studied her expression with intent eyes, like she was exhibit A, and she stifled the urge to squirm in her seat.

'You're really not afraid,' he said, a warm smile curving those lips.

'I have pepper spray in my handbag and grew up in the Bronx.' She tried for an angelic expression.

Calvin laughed and her smile slipped. Every time she heard that sound it felt like he was zapping her with little electric currents. His eyes worked like twin lasers, heating her from the inside.

This was just like what had happened to her mother, except now it was happening to her.

Every conversation she'd had with her mom about boys came flooding back into her mind and dulled the connection with Calvin. Being here with him was risky, even though she'd ruled out physical danger. The last thing she needed was to lose her head and her control when she was with a man. She should leave right now.

'I didn't mean to laugh,' he said, sensing the tension in her. He leaned forward. 'I've never met anyone like you, Shey.'

The way he focused on her was so consuming, she lost the ability to speak. Her imagination ran wild for a second as she imagined herself walking around the table, undressing him and letting him do all the dirty things those eyes promised.

But reality snapped her back to her senses. Shaking her head, she stood, and he rose too.

'Where are you going?'

'This can't happen.'

Shey could tell by his incredulous expression that he couldn't believe she was shooting him down. The reality was that they had no future beyond lunch, and staying for that long would be risky. He was a man used to getting what he wanted, and she had a feeling there were many before her that he'd taken at his will. Scores of women who, no doubt, fell at his feet.

There was no room for a player in her life, messing with her body and giving her what it desired. Accidents happened, she was living proof. But she was smart and learned from her mother's mistakes. Passion led to carelessness and that led to the end of careers. A carefully planned romance that she was in control of would be much safer.

'Sit down. We're just having lunch.'

They weren't and they both knew it. This lunch was a form of foreplay, and damned effective.

'Just lunch?' Shey asked, unable to move. Those truffles were calling out her name, even though she knew a moment on the lips was a lifetime on her hips. He nodded and she slid into the chair.

'Tell me why you panicked. The truth,' he added, like he couldn't stand lies.

His eyes latched onto hers with an intensity she shied away from. She ignored his question. After all, she didn't panic. It was self-preservation, which her body clearly wasn't interested in.

'How do you have a key for here, and why were you at *Storm* on Friday?' If this was the last chance she'd get to ease her curiosity, she had to go for broke.

His grin sent a heated shiver through her, chasing away the last shred of her fear. 'Ladies first.'

Shey stopped the frown before it happened. He was… infuriating really. She reached for her wine and took a sip to calm herself.

'I'm not sure what you expect, but I can't give it to you.'

He picked up his own wine, a calculating glint in his eyes that told her he was looking for another angle to persuade her. Yeah, it was flattering that he wanted her this much, but whatever was between them couldn't go anywhere. She had to keep her focus or she'd be screwed, and not just literally.

'Calvin—'

He leaned forward, elbows on the table. 'Stop fighting me.

15

Maybe I just want to have lunch with a beautiful woman, is that a crime?'

She grinned. 'Is that a line?'

He chuckled and she couldn't help joining in. The tension in her shoulders melted away, and she had to admit the guy was smooth. Either that or she didn't really want to leave in the first place.

Shey glanced down at the plate. He'd bought all her go-to-lunches from her favorite deli. She thought again about the effort he must have put into this meeting. It warmed her heart, especially when she glimpsed the fairy lights above. It was almost romantic. Not to mention over-the-top, since she got the vibe he was only looking to take a dip beneath her panties.

'How about you answer my other questions?'

The air crackled with something taboo, and Shey felt drawn to him like he was a black hole, sucking her in. She tried to fight it, but that was the hardest thing she'd ever done. She needed to keep her head.

'I own the building. Marco wanted to renegotiate the rental agreement to expand *Storm's* offices to this floor.'

Suddenly the effort she found so romantic didn't seem that way anymore. Sure the fairy lights, the candles, and the hamper of her favorite foods, were all lovely. But that was the extent of it. Surface stuff that didn't involve any more effort than picking up a phone and ordering someone—probably Mandy—to do it for him.

'You look disappointed,' he observed.

Shaking herself out of her thoughts, she shrugged. 'I only agreed to lunch to tell you that you're wasting your time. I'm not interested.'

He grabbed her wrist; his hold firm but gentle. Her skin sizzled, and she tried to keep her mind sharp, but all she felt was a stronger pull and she couldn't stop herself from falling into the spiral of urgent desire. He traced his thumb over the veins on the underside of her arm and Shey's breath caught in her throat. Calvin's smile slipped, and his eyes promised things she should know better than to want.

'I think you're as interested as I am, though I seem to be the only one willing to admit it.'

Shey snatched her arm back, his self-assured observation giving her the strength she needed. 'Lust is irrelevant. It'll take more than some sandwiches and wine to get me to swoon over you.'

He picked up some parma ham and cheese with his fingers. 'I don't want you to swoon over me. Eat.'

Calvin popped the food into his mouth. Shey watched that sculpted jaw work as he chewed. She forgot for a second what he'd said. His thick throat bobbed and her heart raced, the pull in every cell of her body intensifying as she wondered what it would be like to lick her way from the hollow in the center of his collarbone all the way up over his Adam's apple.

She reached for the wine and took a huge gulp. It was smooth as silk, just like him. The fruity taste was divine. Not even close to distracting her from his presence, though. He seemed to dominate the entire lobby, his impressive Armani-clad body the only focal point.

'Then what do you want?' she found herself asking, even though she knew.

'You. In a bed. For a few nights, perhaps a week.'

The husky tone of his voice touched her like a caress and his words painted images in her mind of the two of them naked, rolling around sweaty and desperate. She tried to pull herself together; after all, he'd pretty much told her he wanted to fuck her and nothing else, but her body reacted like it was readying itself to welcome him inside, and her mind clouded over.

'I want to do things with you, Shey. Things that will bring us both immense pleasure. I want to fuck you with my tongue, fingers and cock until you can't stand. Then I want to do it all over again.'

Before she could stop herself, his deep baritone voice roused more dirty fantasies. Her clit swelled, her nipples ached and a volcanic rush of hormones vibrated through her. She couldn't

17

breathe, couldn't think of a cutting remark to throw at him to make him stop the assault on her senses.

'Why?' she asked, cussing the fact her voice was all breathy.

His gaze dipped down the upper half of her body, and when he returned his attention to her face, his eyes were wild. 'You are every man's wet dream, Shey Lopez. Curves in all the right places. Gorgeous. I can't not want you. Believe me, I've tried.'

She swallowed.

'And you want me just as much.'

Unable to speak, she stared at him.

That was when he rose, stalked around the table, and offered his hand.

God help her, she placed her hand in his and then she was off the chair and pressed against his chest. Lost in the darkness of his eyes. Lost in the crude words that made her want to spread herself out on the table in offering. He ran a finger up her spine over the silk dress, enticing a shiver and igniting a sharp need at her core.

But that was the problem, wasn't it? Losing control was dangerous. It led to bad things, like the end of a career and accidental pregnancies. The thought gave her the strength to pull away. His mouth opened in disbelief, but she wasn't giving him a chance to let him talk her around again. Shey grabbed her bag.

'Thank you for lunch, but this is a bad idea.'

Her heels clicked urgently across the floor. Just as she was about to turn the lock, he spoke.

'I never would have guessed you'd be uptight about sex.'

Her hand froze on the key and her teeth clenched. She wasn't uptight, just careful.

Then Friday night's conversation flashed into her mind. Safe and controlled relationships were all she allowed herself. Ever. But every cell inside was screaming to turn around and let him kiss her, and maybe more. And why not? She could do crazy, just once, couldn't she? As long as she kept her head, it didn't have to go too far.

Shey turned. Calvin's expression was closed off, but he couldn't hide the heat in his eyes. She dropped her bag, then walked back to him slowly, with an extra sashay in her hips.

'I'm not uptight about *anything*.'

The grin was back as he rested his hip against the table. 'I'll believe that when you stop running from this.'

She stopped right in front of him. 'I'm not running anywhere.'

'What changed your mind?' he asked, but his attention was on her lips.

'I had to prove you wrong.'

He chuckled again, and the noise shivered through her. Grabbing her hips, he maneuvered her until her ass hit the table, and he closed in. Her heart rate spiked, her breath coming in short gasps.

His palms rested on the table either side of her. 'I'm happy to be proven wrong in this case.'

Calvin's head lowered slowly. She closed her eyes, totally lost in the unique scent of him, but still retaining control of herself. His body pressed so close to hers she could feel his erection prodding her stomach, his hard pectorals buffering the soft flesh of her breasts. She was sliding into the erotic moment with him; the urge to let go and enjoy was overwhelming.

His lips brushed her earlobe, soft as a whisper, and she made an incoherent sound in her throat. 'Is this what you want, Shey?'

Shey was trembling so hard she didn't know how to answer. She was wired to him, barely hanging on to reason. All she wanted was to be closer. To have his hands on her. For him to stop talking and fulfill the promises he made earlier with actions.

As if reading her mind, his palms made contact with her outer thighs. The charge that ran through her ignited her senses. She was aware of every one of her pulse points, especially the one aching between her legs. Knees weakening, she grabbed onto his shoulders for support. His lips brushed her collarbone, and her head rocked to the side to give him better access. That seemed to be the reaction he wanted, because slowly he slipped her dress up her hips as he nibbled her throat.

The pull towards him intensified like gravity. The closer she got, the closer she needed to be. His breath tickled her neck as one of his hands slid around to her backside. He squeezed hard and she moaned her approval. Pleasure sparked anew and gathered momentum as it crashed through her. His other hand got to work, sliding beneath her thong, and immediately a long, thick finger entered her. Instinctively, she squeezed her muscles to pull him deeper, ground her hips to get a better angle, and he rewarded her by slipping in another. Though she felt full, it wasn't enough. Shey tried to tell him, then his lips pinched her ear sending a blast of shuddering currents through her body and all she managed was a mewl.

Thrusting his fingers, he squeezed her backside, pulling her into a rhythm that made the burning inside morph to an achy pleasure. The orgasm swelled with the force of a train going full out, and she couldn't bite back the desperate sounds coming out of her throat. His fingers swirled, over and over, barely skimming a spot inside that made heat flash through her. She was panting so hard she couldn't tell him where she needed him to focus, but as she looked at him with pleading eyes, she hoped he understood.

Calvin's jaw was tense and the feral need in his eyes cranked her up higher. She gasped as he hit that spot inside again, and he grinned. Shey let out a wordless protest when his fingers swirled again.

'The anticipation will be worth it, Shey. Trust me.'

She couldn't form a coherent reply, not with what he was doing to her. Taking her body to the edge, then slowing. Finger-fucking her faster as she felt the monumental orgasm slip away, then using lazy strokes right before she could come. She was sweating all over, and with every ragged breath she got another shot of his amazing smell. It was hard to believe that it would be better this way. When he brought her to the edge again and stopped, Shey wanted to weep. Her emotions were as raw as her body, held at the brink, her pleasure and what felt like so much more in this man's control.

This time Calvin slipped in a third finger and started pumping hard. With her nails digging into his shoulders to keep herself upright, she begged him with her eyes for more. Whatever wall he'd put up to restrain himself cracked. His thumb found her clit and his mouth sealed over hers with a growl.

Her control crumbled as everything doubled.

The sensations, the mounting pressure, the electric connection. He thrust his tongue into her mouth at the same tempo as his fingers, and kept that punishing rhythm on her clit until she couldn't breathe. As he sucked her lower lip into his mouth, the pressure exploded in wild spasms, and she grabbed onto his hair to pull him closer, so his mouth could swallow her cry of relief while her body shuddered on.

Shey went limp against him. She felt too open, too raw, more vulnerable than she'd ever been, but she couldn't let him go. Calvin's gentle kisses eased her, reassured her that everything would be fine even though she couldn't think straight. His free hand rubbed up and down her spine softly.

As her mind sharpened, she realized her head had slipped down to rest against his chest, and he still had his fingers inside her. Wedged between the table and him, she was held upright. Shey tested her leg muscles and decided it was better he supported her, but the thought of his hand between her thighs, fingers inside her, made her face heat. Made everything too real. Especially when she realized the pull to him was stronger than ever.

She tried to speak. Her throat was clogged so tight nothing got past except little puffs of air.

Slowly, Calvin withdrew his fingers and her inner muscles tightened on instinct. When they had slipped out all the way, she felt cold and bereft which, she told herself, was insane. Releasing her hold on the silky strands of his hair, she disentangled herself from him, but a hand on her lower back kept her stomach pressed against his straining erection. Her achy core throbbed and pulsed, her muscles clenching with the thought of him filling her up, fucking her as thoroughly with his cock as he had his fingers.

He raised his hand. Those expert fingers glistened and she followed their journey up. Calvin waited until she met his heated gaze, then slipped all three fingers into his mouth and sucked. His eyes closed and an almost feral groan rumbled from his chest. That's all it took for her whole body to fire up again like she hadn't just had the best, most intense orgasm of her life.

When he'd finished his taste test, he stared at her through hooded lids. His eyes burned beneath, but she sensed he had put an invisible barrier back between them again, controlled the emotions he'd let go of when she'd begged with her eyes. It didn't lessen the pull, or the crackle sparking the air between them, but she felt like he'd pushed her away, even though he was still pressed against her.

Not to mention her own self-control was nowhere to be found. God, was she actually considering taking this further? She should have left when she had the chance.

Calvin cleared his throat. 'I need to be inside you. Now.'

# Chapter Three

Calvin's cock was ready to burst through his Armani slacks, and his muscles trembled with the effort it was taking not to pounce on her. Shey's scent—her fucking taste—the way she exploded in his arms, cranked his libido into dangerous territory. Worse still, her silent pleading had shot his control to shreds, letting emotions he usually kept on a tight leash flood through him.

He knew from the second they met that sex with Shey would be intense. The sizzling attraction wasn't one-sided, and it was so much more than he'd experienced with anyone else. It's why he'd broken all his rules and come after her, even knowing the risks.

He had control now, had wrestled it back as he'd nursed her body through the spasms. She'd squeezed his fingers so tight his dick had swelled until it was weeping at the tip.

He hadn't intended to go this far. He'd planned on kissing her, making her admit that she wanted the same as he did. Score a night or two in her bed. Because that's all he could offer her—all he could offer anyone. Commitment was for the weak and he'd already been taken for a fool in that department.

What was between them was more intense than the fire he'd shared with his ex-wife. More necessary than air. Losing control worried him, but the thought of not connecting with Shey on the most basic level was incomprehensible.

'Shey, tell me what you want.' Because he needed to hear her say it, even though she clung to his biceps like she couldn't let go.

'I…' Her eyes swirled like melted chocolate, her cheekbones flushed and radiant. 'We can't do this.' Jerking out of his hold, she knocked the chair over in her bid to escape.

Calvin cursed. He was sick of women playing him to get what they wanted, in Jane's case half of everything he owned. If he wasn't so riled up, if he didn't want her so much, he would have walked away. But there was something there that he didn't understand which was keeping him in the room.

He had to get his cards on the table. 'Quit playing games. We both know this is going to happen eventually. Coy isn't sexy.'

After she smoothed down her lilac dress, she glared at him. 'I'm not playing games, you arrogant ass. I'm telling you I don't want to have sex with you.'

'That's bullshit.' Even now, she glanced down to his groin. 'I don't appreciate being lied to. Tell me what this is really about.'

His arousal had won out over patience, but he wasn't going to force her, silly games or not. Calvin let her pick up her purse and back away to the door. Maybe he should just let her go. She'd lied after all, and wasn't that how it always started?

But he wasn't getting those vibes from Shey. In fact, she was the opposite of all the woman who acted coy around him in the hope of gaining his interest, or his ring on their finger.

'You're a player, and I don't do one-night stands. I'm sorry for leading you on, but that shouldn't have happened.'

His irritation cranked higher. 'I recall saying I wanted you for more than one night.'

Yeah, he was a fool. An idiot walking wide-eyed into another probable femme fatale, but he couldn't find it in himself to turn away. Blue balls notwithstanding, it was hard to ignore the chemistry between them. One night would never be enough to explore that delicious body of hers. To find out what else made her scream. To have her tighten and convulse around his cock and fingers and

24

tongue again and again.

More worryingly, he wanted to find out what happened in her life that made her fight this connection with everything she had. The horrible scenarios in his mind made his blood boil with anger, and kept him by the table even though he wanted to close the distance between them.

As she reached the door, she smoothed her hair and blew out an exasperated breath. 'Do you even have protection?' Shey met his gaze defiantly, and instead of pissing him off it made his dick throb harder.

But shit… 'No.'

Calvin shook his head. He never forgot protection, ever. He glanced down at the tent in his pants with a sigh.

'I could…' Her head bowed for a second, then she met his gaze. Resolve was etched into the sculpted angles of her face.

Calvin raised a brow.

'Return the favor?' Shey licked her lips and his cock jumped.

Trying to think with very little blood in his brain, he worked through all the options. Calvin nodded. 'Tonight, I'll come to your apartment. We can continue where we left off.'

Frowning, she said, 'You can't, I have roommates.'

Was there any easy way with Shey? Calvin didn't think so, and wasn't that refreshing. 'Then you can come to mine.'

He'd never let a woman into his home since Jane, refusing to get that intimate with anyone else. If he went to her place, he could skip the awkward morning-after chit chat over coffee. Something told him Shey wouldn't stick around for that, mostly because he'd want to wake up next to her and fuck her long into the afternoon. The woman was as addictive as she was infuriating.

'I don't think—'

'Don't think about it. Just feel.' As much as he wanted to drive into that sweet, slick body right now, he also wanted her on his bed. Naked. Pushing her over the edge until they were both sweaty and sated.

In the silence that followed he could see her internal struggle: what she knew was inevitable versus whatever ludicrous reasons she had for holding back. Before the latter could win out, Calvin took a pen and company business card from his jacket pocket. He scrawled his address on the reverse, adding his cell number, and handed her the card.

She took it, her hand shaking, and stared down at the words.

'Your lunch break is almost over.' Another reason to wait. 'I'll pack up some things for you to take back to work.' As he spoke, he did exactly that, placing everything in the basket, except the wine. 'I have a meeting soon. Be at that address at seven. I'll even feed you first.'

Shey still had a dazed disbelief about her she couldn't seem to shake. Handing her the basket, he tilted her chin and stared down into the most beautiful amber eyes he'd ever seen, almost laughing when he remembered the starry-eyed quip she threw at him on Friday. He dipped his head and brushed a too-brief kiss on those swollen lips. A current of lust shot through him. He pulled away quickly in case he lost control again and took her against the wall.

He unlocked the door, handed the key to her and left the lobby.

'What about this?' she asked, holding up the key.

Calvin grinned over his shoulder as he reached the top step. 'Bring it tonight and remember to lock up behind you.'

The vision of her standing in the doorway, flushed and dazed from the orgasm he'd given her made his chest glow. Shey hadn't agreed to go to his house tonight, but he would bet his last million he'd see her again.

In fact, he'd make sure of it.

***

As the clock struck seven, Shey knew she was being a wimp. Eloisa was working late and Georgia was held up at a staff meeting. With no one to talk through all the emotions and worries flying around her head, she'd stayed in her apartment.

Pacing back and forth across the shaggy cream rug in the sitting room, she tried to work out what she was feeling on her own. This afternoon had blown her away. She couldn't focus, couldn't do a thing other than go over and over the crazy emotions Calvin had unleashed. He stuck in her head, and she couldn't help wonder who he was beneath Mr. Cool, and it had almost cost her.

Jude had given her another urgent assignment and now she couldn't even remember what it was. But the fact she hadn't got it in on time almost led to a disciplinary. The only thing that saved her job was lying through her teeth, squeezing out some tears, and letting loose some drivel about woman problems. He'd been so uncomfortable he'd let her leave with a promise she'd pull herself together.

There was her first clue that she shouldn't be anywhere near Calvin.

The second was just as threatening to her job. When he'd said he wanted to be inside her, Shey had almost ripped her panties off and laid back on the table with her thighs spread. She'd wanted him inside her too, so much so she'd gone insane, completely forgetting about protection. Sure, she was on the pill and had been since she got her first period, but she *always* insisted on doubling up. Accidents did happen. Felicity had told Shey again and again what having her had cost her in terms of career and a life.

She paused at the huge fireplace and watched the artificial flames dance in the dimming light. Calvin was hazardous to her in more ways than one, but hiding from him was a sign of weakness. She was pissing herself off by not having the guts to go and hand him his damn key back and tell him she wanted nothing more to do with him.

More pacing.

The ring tone of her cell cut off her mission to wear a hole through the rug. The unknown number didn't matter. She knew

27

who it was, though how he got her number wasn't as clear. Mandy had sworn to tell him nothing else.

Shey let it ring, and ring, and ring again until irritation won out. 'What?' she snapped.

'You're late.' The way he drawled the words didn't hide the undertone of frustration.

Well, he could join the club. 'I'm not coming.'

A *tsk* sounded in her ear. 'I thought you owed me one, Shey.'

Oh, that husky voice wasn't fair. She was melting, even though all she had on was her sleep shorts and tank top. She slumped onto the cool leather of the sofa. Unsurprisingly, it did nothing to chill the heat of her skin.

'This has to stop. I couldn't concentrate all afternoon, and nearly got fired.' She had to be firm, had to end this now.

'Sexual frustration does that.'

Her face heated along with the rest of her. 'I wasn't frustrated.' She'd had the best, most satisfying, orgasm of her life.

A low chuckle tickled her ear, like he still had his teeth on the lobe. A delicious shiver ran through her.

'You were, because you wanted me inside you. You wanted my cock to fill you up and make you come, again and again.'

Holy shit. Calvin's words stroked right down to her center and wet heat flooded her panties. Crude words shouldn't have this effect on her. Anyone else and she'd have slammed the phone down by now.

'I can tell by your breathing I'm right.' His heavy breaths sounded through the receiver. At least she wasn't the only one.

'Whether I want you or not doesn't matter. I don't need a man in my life, and this has to stop.' Even if a part of her hated the idea of him giving up on her. Ridiculous. She didn't even know his last name.

'The fact that you don't makes it perfect. If we give in to this spark between us, ride out the pleasure until it's spent, how can that be a bad thing?'

His self-assured tone grated on her, but she knew now he could back up the words. 'I'm not coming over.'

'Then maybe you could return the favor now.'

He didn't mean...

'Slide your hand beneath your panties and tell me how ready you are for me.'

Oh my God, he did.

'Shey, do it.'

'I...' She fisted her hand before she did what he asked. This was—

'Stop thinking. Do you want to know where my hand is?'

*Yes, please tell me.*

'I'm cupping myself, Shey. I'm so hard from the need to be inside you, I can't think straight.' His voice cracked with raw need.

Calvin's honesty sparked something inside her, and a weight lifted off her chest. She was screwing with his head, too. He wanted her as much as she wanted him. To the point where they were both useless.

Her usual defenses melted.

Decision made, she said, 'Squeeze yourself hard on the upstroke.'

He rewarded her with a growl.

Shey reached for the waistband of her yoga pants, wanting to join him in this... whatever it was. Her fingers sought out her smooth mound, then delved lower. She gasped as she came into contact with the burning flesh.

'Are you wet for me?'

'Yes.' She moaned as she tweaked her clit between two fingers, her head falling back against the sofa.

'I want my head between your legs, Shey. I want my tongue where your fingers are, penetrating you, flicking your clit, sucking your sweet juices into my mouth.'

Mindless, she let her fingers take the path he'd described, plunging deep, withdrawing to flick her clit. It was a special kind of torture. She let his smooth voice brush over her, imagining what he was doing with his cock that had him panting as hard as he was. God! She wanted it in her, she wanted—

The sound of keys rattling in the front door knocked her out of the lusty daze. 'Shit.' Shey quickly righted herself as his deep breaths cut off.

'What's going on?' His voice was strained.

'My roommates are back. I have to go.'

His throaty chuckle ramped up the crazed need inside of her. 'We'll continue this another time.'

Shey looked down at her twisted tank top and guessed her hair was just as mussed. Twice she'd had a mindlessly sexy encounter with this man, and she didn't know anything about him. This wasn't her. She didn't do wild and spontaneous. She was careful, always made sure she was in control with the men she was dating. Always made sure she had a clear head.

With Calvin, all bets were off.

The front door opened. 'Shey, you here? We picked up Chinese.'

'I have to go,' she whispered into her cell. 'I'll post your keys back to you.'

'Shey—'

She ended the call before he could talk her into something else. The cavity in her chest got too tight, and she didn't want to think about that. With Calvin it would just be sex, mind-blowing, toe-curling sex. Nothing more. It shouldn't hurt so badly when she decided that things had to stop. He was like a frickin' drug, and after one taste she was on the road to a serious addiction.

Her friends stopped at the edge of the living room when they got a look at her. Their expressions would have made her laugh if she didn't feel so wiped out by all the emotions swirling through her.

'Jesus, Shey. You look like you've been fucked hard and had your heart broken at the same time.' Georgia always did have a way with words.

'Neither.' But it felt like both.

'Come on, I'll set the table. We have some wine in the fridge.'

Eloisa disappeared to the kitchen with the boxes of takeout.

Shey stood on shaky legs and looked down at her cell. He hadn't tried to call back. Maybe this time he'd get the message. And didn't that just sting like a bitch? 'Wine sounds good.'

Georgia eyed her as she made her way to the kitchen. After washing her hands at the sink, she sat across from the two of them at the small breakfast bar they used for eating at after work. It was the same place Eloisa had balled her eyes out over her cheating ex, Georgia had confessed to falling in love for the first time, shortly followed by a gallon of wine when it ended. Now Shey had the feeling it was her turn to fess up with fatty food, her best friends and alcohol as backup.

'Spill it.'

Rolling some noodles around her chopsticks, Shey explained everything that happened with Calvin since Friday. She could only hope Georgia and Eloisa would help take her mind off him.

'I'll never be able to sit on that side of the sofa again,' Eloisa teased when Shey finished.

Shey screwed up her nose, but she was glad for Eloisa's attempt to lighten her mood, and it was working. She dug into the food with gusto, enjoying the chicken chow mein now she'd gotten everything off her chest. Georgia's intense eyes didn't falter, but Shey ignored her friend and reached for the wine.

The silence didn't last. 'I still don't get why you aren't over there fucking him senseless right now,' Georgia said.

Shey almost choked on the wine. Swallowing hastily, she glared at her friend. 'Didn't you hear a word I said? He's distracting me. I can't stop thinking about him, and it's screwing with my job.'

Eloisa piped in. 'I think he's right. You were sexually frustrated. That's enough to screw with anyone's concentration.'

They might as well have slapped her in the face. 'Thanks for taking my side.' Downing the rest of the wine, she tried to fight back her irritation.

'This isn't about taking sides, or your job,' Georgia said, 'this is about Felicity and you know it.'

'My mother has nothing to do with this.'

'Really?' Georgia got up and went to the fridge. She came back with another bottle of white and topped up all their glasses. 'You're so terrified of how he makes you feel, you're pushing him away. Not because he's screwing with your job, but because he makes you lose your head when you're with him. Do you know how many women would kill to feel that sexed-up? Some have never even had an orgasm.'

Shit. 'Georgia I didn't mean—'

'I know,' Georgia's voice grew soft. 'But at the end of the day, what's the worst that can happen? You're not your mother, hell, you're on the pill and even if that didn't work and you ended up pregnant, you wouldn't be alone. You have us. I say you take what he's offering.'

Her hands grew damp and her heart thumped wildly. When her forehead broke out in a sweat, she reached for her glass and gulped down as much as she could.

'Because *that's* why you're afraid to sleep with the guys you like, isn't it? You don't want to accidentally get pregnant and end up alone, putting a baby through what your mom put you through. But you're not her. You wouldn't treat a baby like that.' Georgia's words speared through the pounding in her head.

Panic sucked the sides of her throat together until it got hard to breathe.

'Christ, Georgia, leave her alone,' Eloisa snapped. 'Shey, you all right?'

Squeezing her eyes shut, she fought for composure. Georgia was wrong. It was the worst thing that could happen to any single woman. She knew how hard it was for Felicity to bring her into the world, and knew how much her mother regretted the decision to keep her.

Which, Shey realized, was exactly why she needed an emotional connection with the men she dated. Friendship at the very least.

If doubling up on protection somehow failed, she would know the guy well enough to feel secure asking for support.

Something Felicity never had.

But still, she wanted a career first, then a husband and security before she started a family.

She opened her eyes and met Georgia's steely gaze head on. Her friend was blunt, if nothing else. 'You're wrong. Ending up pregnant to someone I don't even know *is* the worst thing that could happen.'

Georgia shrugged, like she didn't buy it for a second. 'So get to know him.'

'What?'

'If he wants you bad enough, he'll put in the time.'

Shey wasn't so sure about that.

'As much as I hate to admit it, Georgia's kind of right,' Eloisa said. 'You can't go on like this. You need to get Calvin out of your system and if screwing each other's brains out for a week is the only way to do it, then I say go for it.'

The idea of screwing him for a week straight made her flush all over. But she still couldn't get past the sleeping with a stranger barrier, and what about everything else? He didn't just take control of her body and pleasure, leaving her helpless. He cracked her wide open.

'How the hell am I supposed to keep feelings out of the equation?' she asked. 'At lunch today I was in bits.'

Georgia piped in. 'By giving the fling an expiry date. At least then you both know where you stand, and neither of you will build up expectations.'

Shey's mind drifted to the way he had completely controlled her, told her to trust him with her pleasure, and she had. The reward had been the best experience of her life.

She knew he just wanted her body, but she needed a little more of a connection than that. The only problem left was now her second-biggest fear. When she got to know the man behind the suit and cool confidence, would she fall hard and get crushed when their time together was over?

# Chapter Four

By Friday Shey was back into the swing of things at *Storm*. Jude had been pushing more and more of his work onto her, but instead of bitching about it she was grateful for the distraction. Calvin hadn't been in touch, and childishly she'd held onto the key, hoping he'd contact her to get it back. For all she knew he'd replaced the lock to the twelfth floor. Or replaced *her* with someone easier. Shey didn't want to wonder why her stomach felt like it was full of free weights.

After arranging a meeting with a designer for Jude next week, it was almost time for lunch. She was anxious, just like she had been every day this week, to see whether Calvin would contact her.

When a knock sounded at the door, her heart soared, but LB stuck his head through, his expression grim. Well, it was more of an awkward line that had formed on his forehead. Shey resolved to never, ever let someone inject her with botox.

'Everything okay?' she asked.

For a second pain darkened his eyes, but it was gone in a heartbeat. 'I'm taking the afternoon off. Can you hold the fort?'

Shey tried hard to keep her mouth from gaping. Jude was supposed to oversee a photo shoot this afternoon. Though it would take place in the *Storm* building, it was part of a new campaign they had started for page seven and if shit hit the fan, Marco would have both their asses on a plate. The fact Jude trusted her to come up with the goods made no sense at all.

Unless he didn't. 'Is someone else taking care of the shoot?'

That awkward line came back, and his lips turned down at the corners. 'Can't handle it?'

Shey swallowed. 'I didn't say that.' Though she wasn't sure she could.

'Then you're in charge. I'm on my cell if you need me.' With that, Jude left without the usual grandeur.

His shoulders were stooped and Shey noticed his usually sharp appearance had gone. Along with his drive for the job. The thought that he was giving up should make her happy. She had never liked him, but lately he'd been less bitchy and more like a mentor.

Like or not, she hadn't imagined the pain in his eyes. Something was wrong with him, and she wondered if he had anyone else to lean on. LB wasn't a people person.

She didn't have long to wonder. Her desk phone rang, and any hope of a lunch break was quashed. The photographer was running late, one of the models had come down with salmonella, and there was no Jude there to bark orders at her.

Ignoring her rising panic, Shey got to work. She asked Mandy to search the system for a model of similar size and hair color to take over, grabbed the paperwork she needed and made her way to the gallery room they used for shoots. The other models would be antsy, and without LB to keep them in line, she'd have to find a way to pacify them.

By the time the photographer arrived, they were all ready to go. Shey knew exactly what Jude wanted from the pictures, and though she liked LB's ideas, the photographer persuaded her to add a hint of darkness to the shots. It didn't alter the perception much, but enough to show off the labels the girls wore in an edgy way that had much more appeal.

Though terrified of what Jude would do when he saw the pictures, she went with her gut and let the photographer change the style. By the time she got back to her desk just after four, her inbox and voicemail were full. She knuckled down and dealt with everything one by one.

At six her cell rang, and she flipped it open expecting Georgia or Eloisa. 'Sorry, have to take a rain check tonight. I'm going to be in the office for a while.'

'I wasn't aware we had plans.'

Calvin.

Her heart sped and the lull of exhaustion vanished. She remembered the last time that voice had sounded from her phone.

'Friday nights are reserved for the girls,' Shey replied.

'But not tonight, since you're working. Tell me, Shey, have you eaten yet?'

She grinned. He could turn a question into an order and make it sound so enticing she wanted to answer him instantly.

But she didn't. 'What are you doing tonight, Mr. Cool? Other than harassing me at work, that is.'

Another one of those *tsks* that made her vibrate right down to her toes. 'I believe I asked you a question first.'

'I'll grab something later.' Damn it.

His chuckle was rough. Sexy. 'I'm still waiting for my key.'

In those six words, Shey heard the question he didn't ask. The barely contained desire she was trying to hold back. He wanted to know when she was going to break, and she wanted nothing more than to call it a day and take a cab to his place. But they hadn't hammered out the details.

'I will bring it back, but not until we've sorted something out.'

The line was quiet for a beat, then he said, 'Shoot.'

Taking a deep breath, she tried to convince herself that if he didn't want to, it wouldn't matter. The core of what they had was an insane chemical reaction and until it was sated, she wouldn't be able to get him off her mind. Still, the idea that he might not want her enough to go along with what she needed made her hesitate.

'I need more than just sex,' she blurted and held her breath.

Silence.

'I don't mean I want a relationship with you, I know what we have is combustible. But I can't have any kind of sexual relationship with a stranger. Calvin, I don't know your last name, I don't know anything about you, and I need those things to make me feel safe.'

More silence.

A jolt of pain slashed her heart like a whip and disappointment joined the party. This was exactly the reaction she'd expected, but that meant… 'Look, it doesn't matter. I need to get back to work.'

'Wait.' Calvin's voice was hoarse. 'This isn't how things usually go with me. I don't do the dating thing anymore.'

'Why?'

He took a deep breath. 'My marriage ended… badly.'

Shey's eyes widened. 'Oh.'

'Can't we just…' He seemed lost for words.

'Screw? I told you, I want that. But I can't just jump into bed with you. It's not in my nature.'

'I wouldn't hurt you.' His voice was dark, almost a growl.

'I know, but it's just who I am. I need to know the person I'm sharing my body with. After, well, we can put a time limit on it. Make rules. I don't know.'

'Do you like rules, Shey?'

The anxiety melted under a fresh wave of desire. 'That depends on what the rules are, Calvin.' She imitated his tone.

'Fuck. You're killing me, gorgeous.'

Grinning, she said, 'Back at ya, hot stuff.'

He laughed, but it sounded frustrated. 'You win. My cock's too hard for you to justify any protests.'

'Good. It's only fair since I'm squirming on my seat.'

He growled, and it was her turn to laugh.

'Tomorrow night. I'll take you out.' His tone suggested arguing would be pointless.

'What if I have plans?' she teased.

'Change them. I can't… don't make me wait any longer.'

The desperation that leaked through the command played on her own. She couldn't wait either. 'Pick me up at seven.'

After giving Calvin her address, she went back to work with a stupid grin on her face.

*** 

'Did I tell you how beautiful you look?' Calvin asked as he helped Shey into the cab.

Beautiful was an understatement. She looked edible in a tight red tube dress that stopped just above her knees. Even though it hid her cleavage and thighs, the fabric gave him a glimpse of what he was itching to get his hands on. Every curve of her hourglass body was visible, and the dress blocking the view only seemed to heighten the drive to find out what was underneath.

But Shey wanted to get to know him.

It had been years since he'd let a woman know what lay beneath the surface, and her request should have made him bolt in the opposite direction.

When it came down to it he couldn't run, and not just because he wanted her. He wanted to know the woman who was so set on having control in the bedroom, the reasons why she shot him down over and over when it was clear she wanted him just as badly. Hell, he wanted to know Shey; pure and simple.

'That another line?' she asked as he joined her in the cab.

He flashed a grin, then told the driver where they were going. As the car pulled away from the sidewalk, he took her hand in his. The connection between them buzzed stronger, just from the feel of her skin on his.

He couldn't wait to find out what would happen when he was inside her.

'I told you, Lopez, with you I don't need lines.' He brushed a kiss over her knuckles.

'Because I can see through your bullshit,' she said.

He laughed and used his grip on her hand to tug her closer. Shey came along, but she had a guarded expression in her eyes that hadn't been there before. Like she was hiding something, or trying to protect herself from him. Either way, he wasn't going into it now.

He'd answer her questions—within reason—and they could either go back to his place or reschedule for another night. Calvin still had to make sure she understood he didn't do relationships, but they enjoyed each other's company, so hanging out with her wouldn't be a chore. So long as she knew where they stood. He meant what he said when he told her he wouldn't hurt her, and he hadn't just meant physically.

When they arrived at the restaurant and were seated, Shey glanced around like she hadn't seen anything like it. He had to admit, the Italian Bistro was on the romantic side with its antique décor, wooden arches, and ivy-covered stone wall. The lights were dim, the tables lit by floating tea-light candles. Not his first choice for a date because it threw out the wrong message, but the food was out of this world and Shey deserved the best.

The waiter handed them menus and asked what they would like to drink.

'Would you like red wine?' Calvin asked her.

'I'd love some.'

Her smile was so spectacular, he wanted to put it there again. Without turning back to the waiter, he asked for a bottle of Château Lafite, not to impress her, but because he guessed the taste would put that grin back on her face with every sip.

It slid away as she glanced at the menu, then her eyebrows shot up.

'Problem?' he asked.

'It's pricey here.'

Calvin smiled. 'The food is almost as good as spectacular sex.' He laughed as her lips parted in shock. 'Order whatever you want, on me.'

She frowned. 'I can afford to halve the bill, you know.'

He wondered if she would argue if she knew how much the wine cost. 'I invited you here, so it's on me. If you want to treat me to breakfast in the morning, feel free.'

'You're inexorable.'

Calvin grinned. 'I try.'

The waiter returned with a bottle and poured enough for a taste test. Calvin gestured to Shey. She took the glass between her perfectly plump lips. When the wine hit her tongue she moaned in a way Calvin wanted to hear again and again. His cock hardened, his heart sped, and shit, he wanted to drag her away just so the waiter wouldn't get to see the unadulterated bliss on her face.

'Wow,' she said. Her dreamy gaze focused on him.

'We'll take it,' he told the waiter, and when the man did nothing but stare at Shey, Calvin almost lost his cool. 'That will be all.'

The waiter apologized, then disappeared. Calvin filled their glasses.

'What do you want to know about me?' He needed to get this part over quickly, like ripping a band-aid off a wound.

She smirked at him. 'You were jealous.'

He couldn't deny it. The tone he used on the waiter was the verbal equivalent of a slap. 'No comment.'

'I hope you're not starting as you mean to go on.' Shey picked up her menu and he did the same.

He raised a brow. 'You don't seem like the kind of woman who disregards territorial men.'

'All that marking your territory stuff is the fastest way to make me bail on this arrangement.'

Ah, the perfect answer, so why did the word *arrangement* niggle at him? He didn't want her to rely on his jealousy—it would mean she was expecting exclusive, and that wasn't something he could offer. Monogamy on his part had left him high and dry, complete with a broken heart, an empty bank account and little in the way

41

of possessions. He'd never make the same mistakes twice.

When they laid the menus on the table, the waiter returned to take their order, paying too much attention to Shey's breasts. Calvin's irritation breached dangerous levels. When the man left, Calvin prompted, 'Well? You wanted to know more.'

'You were married.'

'That isn't a question,' he said, his tone too sharp, then regretted his shitty mood when she blanched.

'Why don't you just tell me what you feel comfortable telling me?' she asked.

Scrubbing a hand down his face, he reached across the table for her free hand, but she pulled it away. He cursed. 'I'm sorry. I'm not good at this.'

Shey didn't comment, just stared at him expectantly.

'Her name was Jane. We met when I was twenty and still worked for my father. We had an amazing couple of years together, but when my father died the reins of the company passed over to me and I had to spend a lot of time away from her.'

He took a deep breath, rubbed his eyes. It helped that she stayed silent, but he hated talking about his marriage, especially how it ended. 'Back then, we only developed real estate and sold it on. When the economy crashed, I thought it was a safer bet to move into rentals and commercial spaces, like offices, so I bought a few buildings and apartment blocks with the capital in the business. Jane didn't complain when the money started rolling in, but I was never around and that, among other things, pushed us apart.'

'She just gave up on you, when you had all that on your plate?' Shey's frown was harsh. 'That's…'

Since she couldn't find the words, he filled the gap, 'Bitchy?'

Shey nodded. 'Wait, you said other things?'

He met her gaze with a frown. 'None of that is relevant to us. You wanted me to tell you what I feel comfortable discussing, and I have.'

She studied him with a frown of her own, but inclined her

head like she agreed to drop it. Calvin breathed a sigh of relief.

*\*\*\**

Shey bit her tongue against the barrage of questions waiting to burst free. Calvin had said other things caused the break-up of his marriage, and she wanted to know if those things included infidelity. From what she knew of him he was a bit of a player, and marriages didn't break apart because one half had to work day and night for a while. Couples made it through rough patches like that if they wanted the relationship to work.

But what did it matter anyway? She wasn't going to be with him forever, and besides, it might not have been Calvin who played away from home. Still, all she needed was to get to know the man enough to feel like he wasn't a stranger, and she couldn't expect him to tell her things that made him uncomfortable.

'So what's your story, Shey?' he asked, screwing the lid tighter on the marriage topic. 'Any family, friends, ex-husbands…?'

'No ex-husband, and I stay with my two best friends, who're more like sisters than roomies.'

One brow raised, and she suspected he knew she was avoiding the family part of his question like she avoided shopping in Walmart. Shey sighed.

'My mother…' What the hell could she say about Felicity? *My mom wished I hadn't been born.* She so wasn't going there. 'Isn't around. She's the only family I have. Anyway, enough about me, I want to know more about you.'

Calvin grinned in a way that made her think she'd missed something stupid. 'You can't expect to get all that info from me for nothing.'

'You want to know stuff about me?' she asked, and if her tone sounded incredulous she couldn't help it.

After a sip of his wine, he said, 'That's the price.'

Shit. She hadn't expected him to care about who he was sleeping with, unless he was only asking to make the uncomfortable questions stop. In which case, Shey would play along.

'Okay, I'll tell you one thing about me, and you have to tell me something about you in a different context.'

His brows pulled together, but he nodded.

Keeping the perfect poker face, she prompted, 'When you're ready.'

Calvin leaned across the table, those green eyes darkening, and she had to resist the urge to squirm in her seat. 'You don't play fair, Lopez.'

'Neither do you, Jones. The clock's ticking.'

Shaking his head, he leaned back. 'I've told you what I do for a living, that I was married and then divorced. You've told me two things. You owe me one more first.'

Shey pouted. 'Married and divorced counts as two.'

He drummed his fingers on the table, not saying a word. Heat licked her stomach, remembering exactly what those hands could do to her. Calvin watched her carefully, a smile teasing the corner of his lips. The guy knew what he was doing, trying to distract her, and it was working.

But two could play that game. 'Okay, you win.'

Feeling mischievous, Shey took a long sip from her glass, let the berry-flavored wine swirl around on her tongue, and groaned like she'd just had the best orgasm of her life. His jaw clenched and his eyes lingered on her lips. She licked the bottom one slowly, making sure she had him thinking of something other than the conversation.

'I'm great at deep-throating guys,' she informed him in as blasé a way as she could with her insides screaming to be filled by him. 'Your turn.'

Calvin's eyes widened and his jaw dropped. 'Jesus, Shey.'

She shrugged. 'You wanted to make it even, so I told you something. Now I want to know something about you, and, remember,

44

it can't be sexual.' She was turned-on enough for the both of them.

He cleared his throat. Twice. 'I don't know how I can top that.'

The waiter arrived with their order. Shey had been so nervous all day she'd skipped lunch. Probably not a good move, considering she was aiming for sexy and ordering half a cow to devour in front of him wasn't, but she was way too hungry to care.

The second the plate was in front of her, she tucked in. The knife cut through the meat so easily she knew it would be heaven, and when she popped a chunk in her mouth she proved herself right. God, the steak was so tender, it just melted. She was halfway through her meal when she noticed Calvin wasn't paying attention to what was on his plate.

After swallowing down a mouthful, she asked, 'What's up?'

'Do you know how sexy it is to see a woman eat proper food? My cock's so hard it's leaking.'

Holy shit. He wasn't the only one getting wet in the nether regions. 'I…' She inhaled. Tried again. 'Isn't your pasta any good?' Her face heated as she considered all the ways to burn off the joint carbs.

'It's not food I'm hungry for.'

His gaze was so hot she was going to get burned. And yeah, her appetite had vanished. *Let's bounce* was on the tip of her tongue, but she couldn't do it. She'd hoped to get to know more about him, and she could hardly blame him for the detour in the conversation. She'd been the one to kick up the sexy.

'Stop thinking,' he demanded in that oh-so-persuasive voice.

'What?'

He smiled, leaned closer. 'You get this cute little crease between your eyebrows when you overthink things. Stop it. Just let this happen. We have all night to talk, and tomorrow morning. In fact, the whole day if you don't have plans.'

For once she decided to listen to him. All along she'd expected him to have his wicked way with her, then kick her out, and she didn't want to feel like a free hooker. But Calvin planned to spend time with her, non-fucking—unless he was some kind of machine. The rest of her doubts dissolved. Shey looked down at her plate and decided she was done eating.

'Okay, no more thinking.' Smiling at him, she added, 'Will we get the bill?'

He flashed a brilliant smile and she got a little dizzy. 'I'm down with that, gorgeous.'

'Recycling lines?' she asked when he waved to catch the waiter's attention.

Calvin shook his head. 'Just stating the obvious.'

# Chapter Five

As Calvin paid for the meal and they rose to leave, Shey's thighs quivered and her sex clenched. She didn't think she'd ever been so desperate to jump into a guy's bed. The whole week had felt like foreplay. She wanted this hard, fast, and out of control. Then they could get to the other stuff, and do it all over again.

Calvin linked his fingers with hers and she had to hide her surprise. This didn't feel like they were a couple of single people about to fuck. He said they had all night, maybe even tomorrow too. And what was the point in putting a limit on their time together if his bedroom skills were a huge disappointment? Better to know first, then set the rules.

Okay, so she already knew his skills weren't up for debate. More importantly, maybe a week wouldn't be long enough. Shey could wait until after the first round to decide which angle to hit that discussion from.

They almost made it to the exit when a couple strolled into the restaurant. The guy gaped at her like he'd seen a ghost, so she didn't notice the woman on his arm at first. He wasn't much older than Shey, but with nowhere near the sex appeal Calvin oozed. In fact, he looked a bit dull in a drab gray suit with mousy brown hair.

'Shey, my darling cousin, it's been so long.'

She was amazed she even recognized the woman's voice since

it had been almost two years since she spoke to Felicity. The last time she'd run into her mother Shey had played the role of a sister. Obviously Felicity didn't want her to be that close since she had a new toy-boy accessory, but they resembled each other too much to ignore a family connection.

A part of her wanted to play dumb and give the game away, but she didn't have time for this. She couldn't get Calvin back to his place and strip him naked fast enough.

'It has. We have to shoot, but we should do lunch sometime.' Like that would ever happen.

Calvin squeezed her hand, maybe admonishing her for being rude and not introducing him. Or maybe he was as impatient to ditch her mother as she was. Felicity's gaze took her in from head to toe, and when her mother met her eyes again, it was with barely concealed condemnation.

'I didn't know you were pregnant. When are you expecting?' Felicity's voice was tight, restrained.

Oh hell no. 'I'm not.' Her cheeks flamed with anger, but mortification wasn't far behind.

Felicity made a disgusted sound in the back of her throat, while her junior date looked uncomfortable, like he'd been caught up past his bedtime and was trying to think up a good excuse to get away with it.

'I don't care if you are Shey's family,' Calvin said in an icy tone she'd never heard him use before, 'But if you ever bitch at her again, you'll regret it.'

Teen-lover looked like he was about to step in to defend Felicity's honor, but mommy dearest cut him off. 'I apologize for offending you both.' She turned to Shey. 'I've just never seen you so…'

The *fat* went unsaid.

Calvin's hand almost crushed hers. When she looked at him, she had to make an effort to keep her mouth from gaping. He was livid. There was no other way to describe his harsh scowl, or the anger in his eyes.

48

'Wanna get out of here?' she asked him.

He looked down at her, his expression softening. Shey gave him a reassuring smile, but the truth was all the lust had been sucked out of her along with whatever confidence she had. She felt more like a sack of potatoes than a seductress. Felicity had hit her mark, once again.

He nodded, then turned back to Felicity and her plaything. 'I truly hope I never have the displeasure of meeting you again.'

One good thing to come out of this: Shey took a lot of satisfaction in seeing her mother's jaw drop.

The chilly autumn breeze outside cleared her head and helped her purge some of Felicity's poison. All around people were going about their normal evening routines, walking hand in hand with their loved ones, while she was having a rapid-fire shift in emotions. She'd forgotten how catty Felicity could be. Forgotten how much her mom could still hurt her.

But at the same time, Calvin had backed her up, and all those emotions she'd thought she could keep contained came tumbling back. What she needed was to get home, talk this through with the girls over copious measures of hard liquor and chocolate. Lots of chocolate.

Which was probably why she was all hips and ass in the first place.

Instead of hailing a cab, Calvin pulled her into his arms. His rock-hard erection pressed into her stomach and her brain short-circuited a little. Maybe rampant sex would help her sort through everything, but then again, he was part of the problem.

'Don't you dare listen to that cousin of yours, Shey.' His hands slid up her hips, around to her back, down her spine, then cupped her ass.

'This,' He squeezed the flesh in his palms. 'Makes me so fucking hot for you, I can't think straight.' Touching his forehead to hers, he blew out a breath. 'You're so gorgeous I knew from the first second I saw you, once would never be enough. Then you blew my mind when you rejected me, and again when you stood me up. You're the first woman I've wanted so badly that I actually agreed to… date you.'

Shey couldn't breathe right. Her heart was jumping, her mind clouding over, and her hips ground against his. 'My mother, not cousin.'

His confession about craving her so badly made her want to open up, or maybe it was the huge erection prodding into her stomach. 'Felicity Lopez is my mother.'

The anger in those hazel eyes seemed to turn them greener, and his grip on her ass tightened. 'Your fucking mother?'

Nodding, she decided she preferred the cocky Calvin. This version in front of her, all possessive and defending, made Shey want more than just his body. She'd never appreciated anyone standing up for her—she could do that herself, thank you very much—but watching Calvin get angry on her behalf was… a head-fuck really. But nice. Definitely something she could get used to.

But shouldn't.

'Shh. I don't want to talk about her.'

With his arousal for her neon-sign obvious, she was back on board with their original plan. Felicity wasn't going to ruin this night for her. No doubt the second they left, her mother had forgotten all about them.

He stared at her for the longest moment, then shook his head. 'Still want to buy me breakfast?' The smile he offered seemed genuine, but the hard lines around his eyes hadn't smoothed out.

'Depends…' Shey grabbed his open collar, stepped up on her tiptoes and flattened her breasts against his chest. Hmm, maybe open collars were as sexy as ties. 'Whether you make it worth my while.'

She pulled him down to close the distance between their mouths. The second their lips met, the whole world fell away, until she couldn't focus on anything except him touching her. Calvin growled deep in his throat as she continued her assault, pushing

50

her tongue into his mouth then backing off to suck on his lips.

His hold on her ass tightened, and he ground that hard cock against her at exactly the right place, hitting her clit better than any vibrator she'd used. Bolts of heat flared through her, sparking her desire hotter and making her languid. Sliding her arms behind his neck, she pulled herself closer, tighter, and worked her own hips against him. Her breathing was ragged and his *Eau de Pheromone* made her utterly crazy. She wanted her hands on the hot, heavy length of him, wanted it inside her.

Shey moved one arm from behind his neck and slid it down his chest. He caught her wrist just before she reached his belt and abruptly broke the kiss, leaving them both panting. Then reality set in again. They were on the street, with an audience, and she'd been on the verge of orgasm even fully dressed.

'I think we should keep that for when we're alone.' Calvin's voice had serious gravel.

Shey hid her flushed face in his shoulder. 'Oh, God, I can't believe I almost did that here.'

His laugh rumbled through her as his arms wrapped around her waist. It was so unlike what she'd expect from a sex partner, yet it felt so right.

'We need to grab a ride. Now.' Instead of waiting for her answer, he pulled her to the side of the road and waved down a yellow cab.

Shey chanced a peak over her shoulder, and holy shit, they'd drawn a crowd of people. Some tourists, others tutting, but worse, none of them seemed to want to move on. The second Calvin had the door open, she ducked into the back seat.

His slap on her ass stung, but in a way that made her want it again. When he was beside her, she pretended to scowl at him.

'Don't lie and say you didn't like it, or I'll paddle that beautiful golden skin until its pink.'

The threat, delivered in that sexy deep voice, made her shiver all over.

'You wouldn't,' she said, a little shocked that the idea turned her on.

He didn't answer, just cocked a dark brow and gave the driver his address. After a nod, the driver hit the button for the radio and the jazz music that filled the car was so loud she couldn't hear herself think. But she didn't really need to for what she had planned.

Shifting closer to Calvin, she looked at the cab driver. The mirror barely caught her and if he turned around, the front seat would only allow a view of her or Calvin's shoulders. Perfect for what she had in mind. After all, she owed him an orgasm and she didn't like to be indebted to anyone.

Shey threw Calvin a sultry look. His lazy smile and half-mast lids made her think he would be down with the plan. She reached into his lap and went to work on his zip, not bothering with the belt. His eyebrows hit his hairline and he opened his lips on a gasp. She hurried to free him before he could stop her, and had that hot, throbbing flesh in her palm in record time.

Cursing, he darted a glance to the front of the cab and obviously figured out what she already did. There was enough privacy that she could have him at her mercy. Shey leaned in close to his ear, giving his cock a squeeze.

'How long is the drive to your place?' She nipped at the lobe and was rewarded with a grunt.

'Too long.'

Shey slid her palm down his shaft, reveling in the thick veins and solidity of him. She worked him in a twist on the upstroke and he hissed.

'Not long enough,' he said.

Good thing she enjoyed a challenge. Shey paid attention to the glorious cock in her hand. The head was huge, almost red with the blood pulsing beneath. The tip was shiny, and she swirled her thumb through the pre-come, wondering what it tasted like. Calvin's hips jerked and he swelled in her grasp. As if it wasn't big enough to begin with.

Using her free hand, Shey shifted his slacks so she could cup his balls, tightened her grip, and worked him without mercy. His eyes slid shut, his head slammed back against the seat, and his free palm slid under her ass. She was sure if the jazz wasn't so loud, she'd hear his moans.

With every twist in her upstroke, a little more glistening liquid escaped the tip and Shey spread it down over his cock to heighten the sensations. The way his neck strained, breath coming in short needy gasps, and the steely feel of his cock in her hands had her so turned on she had to remind herself they weren't alone so she couldn't straddle him.

The skin of his balls tightened, at the same time he grew diamond-hard. Sweat had beaded on his brow, and he met her eyes with a look of awed lust. Shey brought her finger up to her lips and sucked, making sure to keep her thrusts on his cock steady.

Calvin's eyes popped wide as she soaked her index finger, probably assuming she was imitating sucking him, but Shey had other plans. He was close, she could see it in the tightening of his thigh muscles, and she wanted him to remember this hand job for the rest of his life.

She pulled the finger out of her mouth, then pressed her lips to his to distract him. Shey reached for his balls again, but slid her damp finger lower, over the gland just behind. He gasped into her mouth, and started to pull back, but she wasn't going to let him. Tightening her grip on his cock, she pumped him harder, and slid that wet finger along to the puckered hole. Applying a little pressure, she circled the flesh, all the while pumping him faster.

Calvin's grip on her ass tightened, his free hand fisted on his thigh and his head dropped to the crook of her neck. With his chest heaving, she thrilled at the power she held over him. It was like Monday lunch, only reversed, and it was almost as good.

His muscles tightened, and it was the only warning she got before the creamy liquid pumped over her hand, his shirt, and a little on her dress. She slowed her strokes, nursing him through the spasms and coaxing the last of his orgasm from him.

Slowly, she released him, but he didn't soften as much as she expected he would. Calvin lifted his head, a dreamy, reverent expression on his face, and she winked. Most guys didn't like her touching them there, but with all his talk about variety, she'd known he would be different. She brought her come-covered hand to her mouth, and licked off a little. Her eyes slid shut as the sweet taste of him hit her tongue.

God, she wanted him to come again, in her mouth this time, and swallow everything he gave her.

Calvin pulled her head close and plunged his tongue into her mouth. Everything below her waist went molten and she had to remind herself they weren't alone. And they really ought to clean up.

He was the first to break the kiss and she missed the connection instantly. But he didn't pull back. Instead he untucked his shirt, cleaned her hand, himself, and then straightened up. She looked past him out the window and saw they'd arrived in a residential area with terraced houses.

He pulled her close to his side and spoke into her ear. 'For that, I'm going to make you come so hard you're going to want me to stop, but I won't. Then I'm going to do it again and again.'

The shudder that coursed through her was purely sexual, without even a hint of fear or apprehension. Because she trusted him not to physically hurt her. He made her feel safe, protected, and so turned-on a brush of her panties over her swollen flesh would tip her over the edge.

Shey couldn't wait to find out what he had planned.

*** 

'Can I get you a drink?' Calvin asked when they got inside.

He didn't want to drag her straight to the bedroom and make

54

her feel like she was no better than a one-night stand, even if he was already fully hard again watching her take in his sitting room, from the Italian leather sofas to his tropical fish tank wall separating the room from the kitchen.

Shey turned to him, with a dark twinkle in her eyes. He was on board with whatever filthy thoughts were running through her mind. It was the first time a woman had ever touched him where Shey had, and though he'd almost stopped it, she'd turned an assault on him that he couldn't resist. And was glad he hadn't.

Who knew hand-jobs could be so fucking hot?

'I'd like another taste of…' She made a show of lowering her gaze to his groin.

As much as he wanted her lips on him, he needed his on her more. He hadn't been able to get her taste out of his mind since Monday. Couldn't get her out of his fucking head since she'd brushed him off the first time he met her. Maybe after a few rounds, the chemistry between them would fizzle enough so he could concentrate on work. Calvin wasn't hopeful, but forgetting her wasn't an option.

His reaction to Shey's mother when she'd upset her was proof of that, and maybe more reason to end this now.

'I'm going to clean up first,' he said. His earlier orgasm was drying on his skin and starting to itch. Getting out of the shirt would be a good move too.

By the time he got back to the sitting room in a fresh shirt, he was still aroused and it really didn't help that she stood with her back to him, watching the multi-colored fish. His gaze zeroed-in on that fantastic ass.

He slid his hands around her waist, then up to cup both her breasts, loving that they spilled over his palms. She was all woman, and it was sexy as hell. Her mother—he couldn't believe he hadn't clicked with the resemblance—was crazy to think there was anything wrong with Shey.

Her nipples hardened and he squeezed them.

Shey gasped, pressed that ass of hers into his groin. 'I think you should give me a tour.'

'Anywhere in particular you want to see?' He nibbled her throat, proud of himself for not dragging her off the second she spoke.

'The bedroom.' Her breathless voice cracked the pretense he had on control.

'Then who am I to deny you what you want?'

What they both wanted.

Calvin took her hand and led her through to his room. He half expected her to walk around, checking out the art on the walls or show some interest in the décor like other women had in the apartment he owned before marrying Jane. But Shey only stared at the four-poster bed, a half-smile on her lips like she had an idea his cock would like.

'What are you thinking?' he had to ask. As much as he wanted her naked, he was open to changing his plans.

Shey turned to him. 'Do you own ties?'

'As in restraints?'

Jesus, maybe she was a little more experienced with this stuff than him. But as he thought about it, heat raged through him and his balls hiked up like he was ready to come again.

Some of the lust drained from her expression. 'I can't... I couldn't be restrained.'

He tilted her chin until she met his gaze. Her eyes were wary, and he guessed she didn't fully trust him with her body. It was obvious from their first encounter that she liked to be the one in control.

'I will never do anything you're not comfortable with. Okay?'

She nodded.

Calvin grinned. 'Were you thinking about tying me up?'

That got a laugh from her, and her stiff shoulders relaxed. 'No, I think ties on guys are sexy.'

He'd remember that, and get a few for next time. 'I don't wear them.'

'That's all right. Open collars on you are just as sexy.'

'You've stooped to lines now? Gorgeous, you don't need them to get back in my pants. Trust me.'

Her smile was blinding, and… hell, it warmed him down to his toes. Not in a way that made him want to get inside her. A dangerous way. He needed to get this back on track. Back to what it was supposed to be.

'I'm going to take that dress off you now.'

And he couldn't wait to find out what she wore underneath. Earlier he hadn't been able to feel the line of her thong, and it was obvious she didn't wear a bra.

'Okay. Should I take my shoes off?' she asked.

Calvin looked down to the black peep-toe stilettos. He hadn't noticed them before, which said a lot about the dress on her. And he wouldn't mind those spiked heels digging into him when he was inside her.

'The shoes stay.'

Before she could argue, Calvin grabbed the side of her thighs, just below the hem of the dress. Her skin was soft, almost like silk beneath his palms and he'd bet anything it was the same all over. But there was more than just the texture of her skin he couldn't wait to discover.

He started to slide his hands up, taking the dress with him. Shey grabbed his wrists, stopping his progress, as panic widened her eyes.

'Shey?'

She swallowed. 'I'm… not like other women. I'm—'

'You're gorgeous. Utterly beautiful, so stop thinking.' He took one of her hands and pressed it against his solid cock. 'I've been this hard since you walked out of your apartment, and I'll probably be this hard until I've had you so many ways neither of us can walk.'

Panic dissolved under the flare of lust that flushed her olive skin. Her breath caught and he dropped a quick kiss to her lips. 'Let me see you.'

After she nodded, he dropped to his knees in front of her. He could strangle that mother of hers for destroying her confidence. He didn't want it to ruin this night for her. He would make her feel as beautiful as she was.

Starting at her ankles this time, he caressed his way up her legs, paying particular attention to the spot just behind her knees. When she moaned and grabbed onto his hair, he worked the sensitive spot a little more.

But, like a kid at Christmas, he was too impatient to stay there long, and started to slide the fabric up her thighs. Her legs were everything he dreamed about and then some, with the perfect amount of curves for her frame. Before revealing any more flesh Calvin urged her to widen her stance and nibbled the inside of each thigh.

Her breathing speeded up. He caught the heady scent of her arousal and slow wasn't possible anymore. He shoved the dress up to just below her breasts and did a little gasping of his own.

He was eye level with a pretty purple jewel in her bellybutton. Her skin was flawless and golden all over. But what got his attention was the fact she was completely hairless, all the way down her mound. The tiny slit was covered in her juices, and the urge to taste was so great he'd have to undress her later.

'Calvin?' she asked.

'I…' His voice was so hoarse he had to clear his throat. 'Shey, I need to taste you. Hold onto me for balance if you need to.'

He didn't wait for her answer, instead he licked the smooth flesh. The taste of her, so much better than he remembered, made his cock strain against his pants, but he ignored it. Once he'd cleared the juices, he parted her with his thumbs and nipped at her swollen clit.

'Oh, God.' Her hold on his hair tightened and he grinned.

Then he really got to work. While he held her open, he used his tongue and teeth to tease her swollen flesh, and when the taste started to fade, he'd dip the tip into her sweet center and drag out more. Shey was breathless, and so was he, but he wasn't stopping this until she exploded.

When the muscles of her thighs and stomach tightened, he focused on her clit, keeping up a steady rhythm. Her hips jerked against him, but he didn't try to stop her. This was what he wanted: Shey out of control and lost in pleasure. After the last time he'd made her come, he couldn't get the way she responded to him out of his head.

On Monday, he couldn't do anything with the erotic vision, but he had her here now all to himself, and he was going to do this over and over until the thrill of it vanished and the thrill of her would lessen he hoped.

'Calvin, I'm going to—'

He sucked her clit. Hard. Her cry and the little lump pulsing in his mouth was the most erotic experience he'd ever had. Releasing her, he nuzzled her gently, coaxing little jerks from her just like she had done with him in the cab.

His patience didn't last long, though. Not when his dick was throbbing, leaking and demanding attention.

Kissing his way up her stomach, he pushed the fabric higher, exposing her breasts. Golden too, with dark-pink nipples that stood to his attention. They'd have to wait. He wanted her naked.

'Lift your arms,' he demanded.

Shey obliged and he slipped the dress over her head. Gloriously naked with a beautiful post-orgasm glow, she took his breath away.

'Shey, I'm going to fuck you so thoroughly you'll forget about any other man you've had.' The words were out before he could stop them, and what the fuck did he care if she remembered her other lovers? Monogamy wasn't his thing. Not anymore.

# Chapter Six

Calvin's words shocked Shey out of the post-orgasm high she'd been in. And she wasn't the only one surprised, if his wide eyes and dropped jaw were anything to go by.

He recovered before she did. 'I'm going to hang this up.'

Like someone had shoved a rocket up his ass, he darted over to the walk-in wardrobe and disappeared inside with her dress, leaving her where she was. Utterly naked. Shit. She felt the urge to cover herself with something, but that was ridiculous considering he'd seen all of her.

Something had changed for him. He'd withdrawn again. Maybe after what she said in the restaurant he thought she'd leave. He had said he wasn't possessive, and yet...

Calvin reappeared in the room, with what could have been a lazy smile, but it looked forced. As his gaze slid down her body she felt the heat inside flicker back to life and no longer cared about being naked. She did care that she was solo in this, and she wanted the Calvin back who'd been on his knees before her.

Sliding her hands up to cup her breasts, she said, 'You're still dressed.'

He stalked toward her, his jaw tight with his arousal, and wasn't that sexy as hell? Shey held out a hand, stopping him. 'Strip, then you can touch.'

The smile this time was less forced. More like Calvin.

She paid attention to her breasts, pinching the tips of her nipples and moaning as the sensation shot down to her still-sensitive clit. The guy knew what he was doing, and thoughts of other men hadn't crossed her mind once.

Calvin didn't bother undoing buttons. He whipped the shirt over his head, exposing a rippled stomach, defined shoulders, and, holy shit, biceps that made her mouth water. The belt buckle was next, then he flicked open the button and unzipped his fly in a heartbeat. His pants and boxers fell to the floor together. The man obviously hit tanning salons or had been at the beach lately because his white bits were visible. They didn't make him any less hot.

He was on her so fast she didn't see it coming. His mouth melded to hers with bruising desperation and she was right there with him. Clinging to his biceps, she pulled herself closer. Naked flesh to smooth, hairless skin made the connection between them intensify.

Calvin picked her up and carried her to the bed, still kissing her like he'd die if he didn't. His tongue dominated her mouth, stealing her breath, and when he backed off it was only to suck on her lips, sending shivers of heat through her.

He lifted her onto the edge of the high mattress. With the speed he opened the drawer at the side of the bed, she guessed he was as desperate for this as she was.

Calvin whipped a foil packet out, tore it open with his teeth and rolled the latex down his erection. All the while she watched, fighting the urge to take him in her hands again. The need to have all of him inside her was too hard to ignore.

And then he was kissing her again, with one hand fisted in her hair to tilt her head to the angle he wanted. But it didn't ruffle her control-freak feathers. The sting only intensified the zing in her body. His fingers found her clit again, and it was too soon, she was too sensitive. She tried to squirm away and he released her hair, using an arm to pull her closer to the edge of the bed.

Shey planted her hands on his chest and he slid two fingers inside her. They both gasped, and she clenched her muscles around the digits, needing more to magically appear. She wanted to be filled, and not with his fingers.

'Calvin…' The word was a plea, spoken into his mouth.

He backed off and withdrew his hand from between her legs. 'I know. I wanted to make sure you're ready.'

Ready? She was ten miles past frantic.

Calvin urged her to wrap her legs around his hips, and she obliged. The movement had his erection prodding against her stomach, and God had it grown again? Shey didn't care. She wanted him inside her, and tilted her hips, hoping he'd take the hint.

Instead, he kissed her again, with less force this time. His lips moved like he had all the time in the world, which they didn't. Not as far as she was concerned.

Taking matters into her own hands, she tried to maneuver him to her entrance, but he only thrust enough to put the tip in. Shey bit her lip as Calvin's breath hissed out. This was going to hurt, he was stretching her already, but the pain would be worth it if he knew what he was doing.

'You need a minute.' His voice was tight as he pulled back.

Shey grabbed his erection and used the strength in her legs to pull him close. But he resisted, and she wasn't really a match at all.

'I need you inside me,' she argued.

He laughed, but it was strained. 'Okay. Let me try this again.'

His fingers brushed against her clit, light as a feather this time, and the sensations were extreme. Little jolts of pleasure spilled out from her centre and, as he swirled the tip of a finger around her, heat raged in her stomach, loosening her muscles and preparing for another mind-blowing orgasm.

She grabbed onto his biceps and met his gaze. Those hazel eyes were so dark they looked almost black, but somehow still managed to burn. His jaw had tightened, and the hard lines of his face grew more pronounced.

Then it hit her. He was holding back because he didn't want her to be uncomfortable. Not hurting her was so important to him he was fighting his own urges. And further back, the first time they were alone he let her walk away, sensing her turmoil. He wanted her to feel safe with him. And she did. Implicitly.

But it was so much more than that for Shey. Calvin had done everything she hated a guy doing. She'd bent all her rules for him, hadn't even kicked up a fuss when he'd defended her at the restaurant and the reasoning was becoming too clear. This was more than just screwing, and she suspected it was like that for him too. Nothing else could explain the possessive comment about making her forget other men, and his withdrawal afterward.

But that wasn't what this was supposed to be about. Feelings were dangerous. Feelings made people make bad decisions. It was the only helpful thing her mother had taught her, and made it possible for Shey to keep some sort of detachment from the men she dated.

With Calvin, all bets really were off.

And didn't that give her such chills the building orgasm subsided, leaving her cold.

He stopped, his eyes searching hers until she dipped her head to hide her expression. But he wasn't having that. Not Calvin. He tilted her chin up again and the hard lines of his control were replaced with worry, cracking her wide open.

'Tell me what you're thinking.' His voice was soft, despite the demand.

She wanted to tell him that she was falling for him. That would be one way to make sure they didn't go any further, because he'd done the marriage thing already and she got the impression that road was one he'd never go near again.

'I don't think I can keep this… casual.'

He dropped her chin like she'd given him an electric shock, and didn't that sting like a bitch?

'Shey, I don't do relationships. You know that.' He raked a shaky hand through his hair.

She wished she wasn't so naked. 'I know, which is why I had to tell you.'

He sucked in a desperate breath, like oxygen was going out of fashion, and something in his eyes shifted. It wasn't fear, or anger, or even the disinterest she'd imagined. 'Tell me what you need from this.'

'I don't understand.' Any of it. She'd expected him to insist she dressed and have her in a cab as quickly as possible.

'Do you want exclusive? I can do that.'

'What?' Her blood ran hot again, but it wasn't lust. 'Like you'd been planning to fuck other women while we were together?'

Calvin cursed, and he was lucky he backed off because she was ready to swing for him.

'I'm leaving.'

She didn't get the wardrobe door open. He was right there, turning her around and closing her in.

'I wouldn't have. Couldn't.' The fact he looked surprised by the admission pissed her off more.

'Let me go, Calvin.'

'Not until you tell me what you want.'

Seething, her voice got louder. 'Why, so you can kick me to the curb when you've had your fill and want someone else?'

'I haven't even looked at another woman since I saw you last Friday! When I close my eyes it's you I see, Shey. No one else. It scares the shit out of me.'

Her mouth dropped open and her anger fled. His fear, so like her own, and the brutal honesty in his gaze made it hard to doubt him. She'd been right: he was in the same place as her, and somehow that made what she felt only half as scary. But taking this further now could push them both over the edge, until they were somewhere they couldn't come back from.

Shey placed her palm against his chest, feeling the warmth of his skin, the crackle that suffused the air between them, and she knew walking away now wasn't an option. Her response to him was so great, so immediate, it could burn her.

Or could turn into the best night of her life. She wanted to find out, and figured she'd survive the rest.

'We need rules so this doesn't get out of hand,' she whispered.

'Rules?'

Shey swallowed. 'Yes, rules to keep us both from falling.'

Since she was halfway there the rules would have to stop her falling harder, or let her get away before it became too much.

'Let's hear them, then.' His hard tone suggested he wasn't happy and she couldn't figure out why.

'We can only do this for two weeks, then it has to end.' One week just wouldn't be enough.

'Fourteen nights, whether we spend them all together or over a longer period,' he countered.

Spending them together would get them out of the way, but it would be so intense having a day or two off wouldn't be a bad idea. 'Deal. And neither of us can sleep with anyone else in that time.'

He scowled at her, 'I told you—'

Shey covered his mouth with her hand. 'I know, and I believe you. I just want you to know I won't be seeing other guys either.'

His hard body relaxed and he slid his hands onto her hips, stepped closer. Her body melted, feeling how ready for her he still was, with his erection standing for her attention. But he didn't make a move to rush her along with her silly rules, so soon after they'd almost got down to fucking, and that, more than anything, made her realize he was taking her seriously.

'Any more?' Calvin asked.

Shey shook her head.

'Do you still want to leave? Try this again another night?'

The fact he could give her that option when it was so obvious he wanted her made her regret stopping what should have happened. 'No, and I'm sorry I freaked out.'

His grin lit up those hazel eyes and left her breathless. 'Thank

God. I think my balls would have fallen off if you left.'

She cupped them in her hands and he hissed through his teeth. 'Still feel attached to me.'

'Two can play the teasing game, gorgeous.'

She was about to apologize, but his mouth came down on hers hard and hungry as his fingers slid inside her. She groaned into his mouth instead and he took advantage, sliding his tongue in with the same slow, steady thrusts he made inside her.

Shey released his balls in case she hurt him and instead grabbed on to his solid biceps for support. Calvin flattened her against the door with his big body, squashing her breasts against his smooth chest. His thumb found her pleasure center at the same time his fingers found that place inside that changed everything. And he knew, whether it was from experience or the fact she clenched hard around his fingers. He kept rubbing that spot inside, over and over with increasing pressure, until all she could do was try to breathe right.

The pressure built higher, faster and more intense than anything she'd experienced. His strokes outside and in were enough to push her pleasure further, beyond any peak she'd known, but it didn't knock her over the edge. Tears welled in her eyes at the exquisite agony he inflicted.

Trapped in a prison of pure pleasure, whimpering was the only thing she could do.

'I'll be inside you when I let you come. I want to feel your body squeeze my cock.' His voice was hoarse and his breath blew against her face.

'Please.' It was the best she could manage.

Calvin withdrew and she almost sobbed, but he picked her up, wrapped her legs around his waist and entered her in one long, easy stroke. Shey's lids slid shut, feeling every inch of him invading her sensitive channel. It was too much, and yet somehow perfect.

'Look at me, Shey.'

She did, and saw he was back to fighting for control, but his eyes were filled with more than passion. The connection between them wasn't just sex, and he must feel it too, why else would he look so wary?

'Fuck me, Calvin I need—'

He did, hard and fast. Filling her completely, then pulling out almost all the way. Her back hit the cupboard door and every stroke dragged the thick head of his cock over the place his fingers had stroked. The sensations were so much more than that, because she was full to bursting and the look of pure bliss in his eyes revved her higher.

Shey held onto him, squeezed her muscles around his cock and tried to make it even better for him. Show him how good it was for her.

With their bodies slicked with sweat, the smell of what she thought was aftershave was stronger, and she realized that it was just him. The perfect scent, her perfect everything.

Then thinking became impossible. The pressure built and built until she couldn't breathe, until she didn't know if she'd survive it when the orgasm hit her. But Calvin didn't give her time to worry. His expert strokes hit that sensitive place in dragging thrusts, getting faster and harder.

One of his fingers slid around to her other entrance, one she'd never allowed a man to touch, but he wasn't anyone, and she trusted him with her body. The pressure on the tingling skin drove her higher, and as his gaze intensified on her his cock hardened inside.

Then he slipped the tip of his finger into that dark place.

Shey exploded in a rippling tide, her whole body going into a mindless seizure of pure ecstasy, and her vision went dark. She couldn't hear over the sound of her own heartbeat in her ears, and had the vague sense of Calvin's lips on her neck, but only because it caused more pleasure to shoot through her.

When he stilled, and the crashing waves steadied, she went limp in his arms. He was still deep inside, not completely hard but nowhere near flaccid, and he looked at her like he'd never seen her before.

'I…' Calvin swallowed. 'Sweetheart, that was…'

Yeah, Shey didn't have words for what it was either. And she didn't care. Exhaustion made her lids heavy, but that was crazy. She'd hardly done any work.

'I know.' Her eyes closed and she had to force them open again. 'Can we go to bed?' Staying up and getting to know him didn't seem possible as exhaustion clouded her vision.

He carried her across the room, not withdrawing from her until the covers had been pulled back. After removing her shoes and tucking her in, he dropped a light kiss to her lips, then disappeared into the bathroom. Shey's lids slid shut and she wondered if it would be better if she went home, but getting her legs to work didn't seem possible.

But then Calvin came back. The bed dipped under his weight and she rolled over to get closer. He still smelled like sex and that fantastic scent of his had intensified. So much so that she felt another stirring of heat in her stomach, but she wasn't in a fit state to go at it again.

Pulling her close, Calvin stroked her hair and she kissed his chest. Neither of them spoke as they lay there, and Shey guessed that was because there really weren't words to describe what had passed between them. Sex had never been like that for her, ever, and she suspected not for him either. Two weeks of this and she'd be lost to him. Shey knew it.

But the usual fear didn't come and, as she drifted into a blissful coma, she couldn't think of a better way to go.

# Chapter Seven

Even though he'd barely slept, Calvin was awake early. The room was still dark, and as he lay on his back watching the ceiling, he tried to figure out why he liked Shey's head on his shoulder and her arm around his waist as much as he did.

By all rights he should have felt trapped, suffocated even, but instead he was stroking her hair, reveling in the feel of her soft exhalations against his chest. He was afraid to wake her to break this moment of intimacy, a moment he usually avoided like the flu.

Shey stirred, and her eyes opened halfway. 'Hey.'

He smiled down at her. 'Hey.'

Then her eyes shadowed and she pulled back her arm. Instinctively, he held her close.

'I'm sorry, I didn't mean to… ' Panic flickered across her face.

'Drool all over me?' Calvin teased. He hated that she felt any kind of fear around him. 'I don't mind.' He winked.

Shey shook her head with a smile and snuggled back into him. 'I don't drool.'

'Really? Tell that to the pool of saliva on my shoulder.'

She smacked his side gently and he laughed.

'You're such a cocky—'

He pressed his mouth to hers, cutting off whatever insult she was about to throw his way. Her lips were rigid at first, but as he slid his hand down her spine, cupped her backside, she melted into him. Heat flared in his groin and he pulled back. Though her eyes had darkened and he had no doubt she'd be up for round two, it had obviously been a while for her and he hadn't been gentle last night against the door.

'How are you feeling?' he asked, using his free hand to sweep velvet hair back from her face.

Shey pouted. 'Deprived.'

'Later, I promise.' He dropped a quick kiss to her nose. 'You owe me breakfast.'

'I'm not going to breakfast in last night's dress. Talk about the walk of shame.'

He hugged her closer. 'I don't mind breakfast in bed.'

'Lumpy pancakes it is,' she said.

'You can't cook?'

The fire in her eyes as she glared at him told him he'd put his foot in it.

'No, not all women are born with that gene. My mom didn't think I needed to learn, since she didn't see much point in eating anything that wasn't pre-prepared for her with a tiny calorie count.'

Anger at her mother burned through him in spades, and not because he was sexist and deigned all woman should be tied to a stove, but for the way that drainpipe treated her daughter.

He'd been lucky. His father had always made a point of being there for Calvin and supported him through everything.

'Your mother doesn't deserve to call you her daughter.'

Her eyes widened, but she shrugged. 'Sometimes I think that, but she prepared me for the real world better than anyone else could have.'

Calvin's doubt must have leaked into his expression, because she sighed.

'She told me I could only rely on myself, that if I wanted a career and the best things in life, I had to work for them. She said that if I let my heart rule my head I'd end up like her, a young single mother whose career was put on hold.'

This time it was rage that burned through him, so acute he couldn't hide it. Shey studied his face, but didn't speak. He couldn't, not without cussing out her mother. Instead he untangled himself, and crossed to the ensuite.

'I'll make us pancakes,' he said, and shut the door.

***

Perched on a chair wearing nothing but a shirt Calvin had given her, she sipped her coffee and watched him expertly beat eggs in a bowl. He'd thrown on a pair of black boxers that really didn't do much to disguise that fantastic ass of his and for the first time in her life, Shey was up for skipping a meal in favor of taking him back to bed.

She couldn't believe he'd gotten angry again over Felicity. It just confused her more. He'd made it clear he was closed off to emotions, which was why she'd panicked first thing. Snuggling felt like breaking rules, but he hadn't seemed to mind. Either that, or he saw how freaked out she was and tried to reassure her. Still, this was starting to feel like more than two weeks of sex should.

Shey needed a distraction. 'How did you learn to cook?'

He poured some of the batter mix into a pan on the stove. 'My father taught me when I was young. He was great in the kitchen. Had to be after my mother died.'

'I'm sorry,' Shey said.

Calvin shrugged, but didn't turn from the stove. 'It was a long time ago.'

She watched the muscles work beneath his smooth, bronzed skin and wondered if losing so many people in his life was another reason he thought it was better to go it alone. Not that it should matter, she reminded herself. Mind-blowing sex fizzled out, and Calvin had already said he wasn't the guy who could promise

71

monogamy or a relationship. She wondered if his ex-wife had killed that part of him, or if it was his own actions that did it.

She didn't ask any more questions as they ate, and Calvin remained silent. The air between them still crackled, but in an uncomfortable way. She didn't want this fortnight to be filled with mornings like this. The sex had been good, but—

'So, tell me what you like to do with ties, Ms. Lopez,' Calvin said with his sexy wry smile.

The tension seeped out of her shoulders and she grinned. 'Buy some and you'll find out.'

The idea of restraining him with the silky creations and having her wicked way with him made a hot flush flare through her body.

'I think it's time for a shower, don't you?' he asked, his eyes dark and delicious.

Shey placed her cutlery on the table next to her empty plate. 'I *am* feeling dirty.'

Calvin was out of his chair, around the table, and hauling her willingly to the bathroom at record speed. Excitement unfurled in her stomach as she kept up with him.

\*\*\*

The days went by too quickly for Shey and Friday rolled around before she knew it. She had plans to hit Club Zero tonight with Georgia and Eloisa, but she couldn't fight the ache of wanting to see Calvin again.

Sex with him was so intense, so erotic, she couldn't think straight. Together they were mindless, primal and it was turning out to be addictive. A night off was exactly what she needed, but like a true addict she was already having withdrawal symptoms. She eyed her cell phone on her desk, and told herself she was *not* calling him to hear his voice.

But it wasn't a battle she'd win easily. When lunch time came, she grabbed her purse and left her cell on her desk. Remove the temptation and she'd be okay.

Until she found the ultimate temptation at the reception desk talking to a blushing Mandy.

Not that she could blame Mandy. Shey blushed a lot when he turned the charm on with her, too.

His attention zeroed-in on her and made her hot all over. He had this way of making her feel like the most sexual woman who ever existed, and that was exactly how a man should make a woman feel.

After murmuring something to Mandy, he crossed the foyer toward her.

'What are you... Oh my God, is that a tie?' Black silk was knotted around his throat and her knees wobbled.

Calvin's grin said he was enjoying teasing her. 'Do you like it?'

Before she could answer, he pulled her into an embrace and his mouth crashed down on hers. Shey clung to his shoulders as she was swept away in him. Pressing herself closer, she felt the stirrings of his arousal pressed against her thigh, which only added to the fire inside.

He pulled back enough to look at her face and cupped her cheek. 'We have an audience,' he whispered.

Shey's eyes widened as she looked past him to see Mandy and LB with gaping mouths. Oops. She squeezed her eyes shut and he laughed.

'Lunch?' he asked.

'Please.' She'd have agreed to anything to get out of there.

Since he'd worn a tie, Shey expected they would be taking a trip to the twelfth floor. When he pressed the ground button in the elevator, she frowned at him. A half-smile curved his lips, and she decided to hold back her questions. After all, he wore it for a reason and she'd find out soon enough.

But he only took her as far as her favorite deli and told her to grab a seat. She did, and tried to keep the disappointment she was feeling from her expression. She wasn't a nymphomaniac, and the fact she was acting like one pissed her off.

He returned with the sandwiches and a couple of coffees. 'How was work?'

Shey couldn't keep her mouth shut. 'Why are you doing this?'

He had the gall to look taken aback. 'Doing what?'

'Turning up here in a tie and taking me to lunch.'

Calvin's husky laugh shivered through her. 'I bought the tie for tomorrow, and I'm taking you to lunch because I won't see you until then.'

She stared at him with wide eyes. The words didn't sound like a man who wanted just sex, and he must have realized it because he cleared his throat and picked up his sandwich.

'Eat up, Shey. It's your favorite.'

She did, barely tasting the chicken or Dijon mustard. Last week she'd been the one who wanted to get to know him more so she would feel comfortable with him, but he'd been learning things about her too. Like how she couldn't stand Jude, but felt sorry for him because he seemed to be going through a rough patch with his husband, that Eloisa and Georgia were like her sisters and she couldn't imagine what her life would have been like if they weren't there, and he even knew about her mixed feelings toward Felicity.

And now he was having lunch with her because... what? He missed her? This felt like breaking the rules, crossing boundaries both of them had put up.

He smiled at her, and the genuine warmth in his eyes made her heart flutter. Crap. Things were changing, and she didn't know if she was strong enough to stop herself from falling for his charms. And where would that leave her? High and dry in two weeks, with a broken heart.

She put the unfinished sandwich down and pushed her plate away.

'Shey?' he asked, concern making faint lines on his forehead.

'This isn't what we agreed, Calvin. Lunch wasn't part of the deal.'

His expression closed down and he nodded. 'It won't happen again. I only thought the anticipation of seeing what I bought now might heighten things tomorrow.'

He didn't meet her eyes through the lie, and she didn't call him on it, because a part of her wanted him to miss her. That wasn't part of their deal either.

'You know, I'll make you pay for teasing me,' she said, in an attempt to ride over the awkward.

Calvin smirked at her. 'Do tell.'

Mr. Cool was well and truly gone now, thank God. 'I may use it to tie you to your bed and have my wicked way with you.'

He leaned closer, and she caught a lungful of *Eau De Pheromone*. The air crackled between them, and she had to squeeze her knees together to calm the ache between her thighs.

'And how exactly would that be a punishment?' he asked, back to his cocky self.

Shey leaned so close her lips were almost touching his. 'Because it will be up to me if I let you come.'

He caught her lower lip between his teeth and used it to tug her closer to him. The sensations shot right down to her center and she groaned. He released her, then dropped a light kiss on her lips.

'Try it, but I'll have to return the punishment. Fair's fair.'

She swallowed at the threat, but the usual panic didn't come. In fact, the idea of giving up that much control and being at his mercy only made her hotter, and her cheeks flushed. Calvin studied her reaction, then his mouth tilted at one corner.

'You trust me enough to let me take control.'

It wasn't a question, so she didn't feel the need to answer. Plus, he looked thrilled by the realization, so she couldn't let any of the sly remarks running through her head out.

Calvin ran his fingers through her hair. 'I won't ever take advantage of that, Shey.'

'I know, and I'd never take advantage of your trust either.' The distant look in his eyes made her suspicions about his marriage niggle until she couldn't hold back her curiosity. 'What happened with Jane? You can tell me, you know.'

His jaw clenched, and he removed his cell from his pocket and focused on the screen. 'She took almost everything when she left.' When his gaze met hers, his eyes were cold. 'I'm sorry, but I'll never allow a woman to do that to me again.'

What happened must have been bad, and now she wasn't convinced the separation was down to him. Did he end up broken-hearted? That would make her understand the person he had become.

Or *was* this who he was, and his wife had caught him in an unpleasant situation?

His thumbs moved rapidly over the cellphone keys. He'd never done that in her company before and it felt like a brush-off. She should leave. Better than sitting there feeling unwanted.

'I should get back to work,' she said.

Calvin lifted his head, leaned forward and pressed his mouth to hers in a sweet, unhurried kiss that made her tingle all over and left her wanting more. When she opened her eyes, his burned with something deeper than lust, brushing over the disinterest. Shey guessed he wasn't the only one looking like they wanted more. She was feeling a little more than desire herself.

\*\*\*

Calvin wasn't a man who gave up control easily in the bedroom, and didn't think it would be something he'd ever enjoy. With a wrist secured to each bedpost, blindfolded, and Shey teasing him with her tongue and fingers, he had to revise his initial opinion.

'So, are you sure anticipation is worth it?' she whispered into his ear.

His erection swelled, begging for her attention, but of course, she paid it none. The minx. 'I'm sure it will be. Shey, get up here.

I want to taste you.'

'Topping from the bottom?'

He laughed and the bed dipped as she climbed on.

'Take off the blindfold,' he commanded.

'Nope, I like having you at my mercy.'

She straddled his hips and her hot, soaked entrance slid across his erection. Calvin groaned. His hips thrust without his permission, and the tip penetrated her. Shey froze above him and he gasped. She was so hot and wet. Glorious.

'Calvin, we need… '

He pulled out, his breath sawing through his lungs. 'I know. I'm sorry.'

'It's not because I don't trust you, I do. It's just— '

'You don't have to explain. Pregnancy wasn't part of the deal.'

Referring to what they had as a deal burned his throat on the way out, but it's how she saw their time together and he had to remember that. It was getting too easy to be with Shey, in or out of the bedroom. So much so that yesterday he'd wanted to meet her for lunch because he wouldn't see her until tonight. But she was right to call him on it.

'I'm on the pill, but the idea of getting pregnant terrifies me, so I always double up.'

Calvin gritted his teeth. Her sorry excuse for a mother didn't deserve Shey.

'Take off my blindfold.'

Something in his voice must have told her he wasn't playing around because she did. Her expression was closed off, but she couldn't hide the pain in her amber eyes. His lungs shrunk until it was hard to breathe.

In a gentler tone, he said, 'Untie me.'

Shey did as he asked. As soon as he was free, he crushed her against his chest. 'I understand, sweetheart. It terrifies me too.'

He kissed her then, soft as a whisper, and took his time. Felicity should be burned at the stake for how insignificant she made her daughter feel, and Calvin made it his mission that night to show Shey exactly how special she was. For the first time in years, he made love to a woman.

# Chapter Eight

Staring at the computer screen, Calvin couldn't even pretend he was interested in the quarterly statements his accountant had prepared. Before, he'd needed to make money to keep Jane happy. After, when she'd cleared him out of almost everything, he worked hard to pay off the loans he'd taken out for the divorce settlement.

Now he didn't give a shit what he was worth. He suspected Shey didn't either. Not at this moment.

All she wanted from him was two weeks of sex with someone she felt comfortable with. Which he'd been happy with initially. Enough time to scratch the itch, burn out the chemistry between them, and go back to his life. But it was backfiring on him. Every touch, every kiss, every time her tight body clenched around his, it only increased his need for her.

And waking up with her in his bed was a different kind of addiction one he wasn't sure how he was going to break. Wasn't sure if he wanted to, but what could he offer her, really? He refused to marry again, and as independent as Shey was, he knew that sometime in the future she wanted the things she didn't have growing up.

Instead of that insight putting the chills on his libido, it infuriated him because the person who gave her those things wouldn't be him. Shey gave him her trust and he would show her every day how grateful he was, but it wasn't a favor he could return. Not that it mattered. They only had a few nights left together.

Calvin didn't want to examine too closely why that realization filled his guts with dread.

His desk phone rang and he hit speakerphone. 'Not now, Mary.'

He had no appointments that afternoon and he wasn't in the mood to take calls.

'I have a woman here to see you.'

Calvin cursed. 'I don't have time for this. Tell her to come back another day.'

He cut off the intercom, deciding to pull his head out of his ass and get on with work. Why bother torturing himself over something that wasn't meant to be? He had his business, the one constant in his life, and if he didn't pay attention he'd lose that too.

His office door opened. 'Mary, I said— Shey?'

'I know you're busy, this won't take long.'

She closed the door behind her and hurried over to his desk, a pure vision in a purple shift dress with matching heels, not unlike the ones that left marks on his ass and back last night. His cock hardened with the memory.

But it wasn't what she wore, or how gorgeous she looked with her hair and make-up expertly done, that turned him on so much. Without it all, she was just as stunning. It was Shey, pure and simple, and a few more nights were never going to be enough.

'What are you doing here?' He rose, rounded the desk and pulled her close. 'Not that I'm complaining.'

She smiled. 'Marco wants to see me tonight. He says it's important and I don't know how long it will take, so I might not be able to come over.'

She looked confused, but happy. Almost blissful, in fact, at the prospect of meeting the bastard. Calvin saw red. 'He wants to *see* you? At night? After office hours?'

Her eyes widened. 'It's nothing like that. Marco's married.'

'A ring on someone's finger doesn't guarantee loyalty,' his voice was cold; surprising since the heat of his anger was scalding.

Shey pulled away from him. 'Some men know how to keep their dick in their pants.'

That she assumed he was talking about himself only made him angrier. He hadn't cheated on Jane, or any other woman. Jane had, and her affair was something he'd kept to himself. Nothing like his wife seeking another man's body to put a dent in his pride.

But Shey *knew* him. Better than anyone. For her to think that he would after his promise infuriated him. 'I suppose I'm in the category of those you deem incapable? Haven't we already been through this?'

She looked startled. 'I'm sorry. I didn't mean—'

'It doesn't matter.' Or it shouldn't, but it pissed him off that she thought so little of him.

'Look, I have to go. I have a meeting with a designer a block away. I just wanted to see you in case I couldn't tonight.'

'I thought that wasn't part of the deal?' The second the words left his mouth, he regretted them.

Her eyes turned shiny. 'You're right. I don't know what I was thinking.'

Shey turned to leave. Everything in him wanted to stop her, but he couldn't. He'd already broken his own rules for her twice, allowing them to become more than a casual affair and again, agreeing to her time limit. Chasing after her now would only show her she had him by the balls, just like Jane had.

'Shey, you fuck Marco and our *agreement* is over.'

She turned to him with wide, shiny eyes and the blow on her hit him as hard as if he'd stuck a knife in his own chest. His anger dissolved and he cursed. He stepped closer and she pulled the door open.

Fuck. 'I didn't mean that. I'm sorry, I know you would never—'

'Go to hell, Calvin.' The door closed behind her and he slammed his forehead into the wood.

The anger he was feeling wasn't at her. He'd been frustrated since

81

he took her to lunch on Friday. Frustrated because he was falling and he couldn't let himself. Pissed off because she saw what they had as a deal, nothing more. But he shouldn't blame her for any of that, since he had stated at the outset sex was all they'd have.

He'd find a way to make this up to her, he had to. But then what the fuck was the point? They were going to end after a few more nights together, and forgetting about Shey would only be harder as time went on. If he didn't rip her out of his life now, later he'd find more excuses for them to stay together longer; other reasons to delay the inevitable. Maybe letting her go like this, angry and thinking he was a bastard, was the best way.

Even if hurting her tore him up inside.

***

Shey didn't have much time throughout the day to worry about the meeting. She seethed at what Calvin had thought her capable of. After she'd gotten so mad on their first proper date because she thought he'd be sleeping with other women, he had the nerve to accuse her of considering doing the same.

Well, like he said, a ring on his finger didn't ensure he'd stay faithful, so why should a couple of rules make a difference? Then he had the gall to ask her if she believed he would cheat? The bastard.

Although he never mentioned cheating on Jane, she couldn't be sure. He'd said the marriage ended because they were pushed apart by his job, but 'amongst other things'. What was she supposed to think?

Taking a calming breath that did absolutely nothing to ease the fury inside, she fixed a smile onto her face and opened the door to the exclusive men's club Marco had invited her to. Giving her name to a guy who looked like a pro wrestler, clad in black with an earpiece, she wondered what the hell it was she'd stepped into. The man escorted her through the club, and every table had the refined types she'd imagine were better fitted to England than a place like this.

The décor had an old-English feel, the wood and furnishings expensive, and it didn't take long to work out she was the only woman there. What the hell was Marco playing at? A sinking feeling weighed her down. If Calvin was right, where better to have an affair kept secret than in a place no women could enter.

Shey was about to turn on her heel when she spied Marco. He wasn't alone. Her chin dropped when she saw the little bitch to Marco's right drinking what looked like brandy and smoking a cigar. LB wasn't clad in his usual gothic style either. He wore a suit, plain and dull and so unlike him she wondered if it was his older brother, but when she got closer and they both rose, Jude's gaze ran over her outfit in that disapproving way of his that reassured her he hadn't had a complete personality transplant.

'Shey, I'm so glad you could join us.' Marco pulled out a seat and she slid into it.

She wanted to ask what was going on here, but Marco was the big dog and she was LB's assistant. She had as much right to question him as she had to be there, and the latter was only because Marco allowed it.

'Thank you,' she said.

Jude shifted in his seat and finished his drink in one go. The place obviously made him feel uneasy, and she could understand that. Worse, LB probably knew why she was there, so he couldn't be as uncomfortable as her. But another good thing mommy dearest had taught her was the perfect poker face, and Shey embraced it now.

'I trust you are well.' Marco didn't look like he cared either way.

He was obviously stalling with what he probably assumed was polite small talk, but she was sick of being treated like shit by men. Jude, Calvin, and now Marco. Straightening her shoulders, she met his eyes steadily.

'Why am I here, Marco?' Demanding things of the owner of

*Storm* was a bad idea, but she'd rather he fired her on the spot than patronized her with bullshit.

His eyes widened for an instant, then he laughed. 'Jude's right, you've got balls. Those will serve you well in this business.'

She sneaked a look at Jude, surprised he'd even mentioned her to their boss, but his attention was fixed on his empty glass. He didn't look happy. That wasn't a huge surprise, but if she was brought here to be canned and LB was there, she assumed it would be for his enjoyment.

'I want to make you an offer,' Marco said, dragging her attention back to him. His expression was hard to read. 'Jude here is going to head the launch of a new magazine being released in autumn. For this he'd be assigned another assistant.'

Shey tried to hide the panic threatening to close her throat. 'What about the current article on page seven?' Were they at least going to replace Jude, or cut the space for advertising and leave her without a job?

'That would be yours, if you wanted it,' Marco said.

Shey couldn't stop her mouth from falling open.

'And of course you, would be assigned your own assistant. Jude assures me you're more than capable of managing the feature, and what you did last week with the shoot was extraordinary.'

She was dreaming, that must be it. Things like this didn't happen to her. LB wouldn't recommend her for the job. And why bring her here to offer her a promotion? Surely the office would be a better place to meet.

Unless… 'What's the catch?'

Marco laughed again, an uncomfortable rumble that only increased her suspicion. 'Jude's right; you catch on quick.'

'I learned from the best.' And when she threw a pointed look his way, he still didn't meet her eyes.

'As you know, we're leasing the top floor. Jude will be moving there. The new magazine will be a smaller weekly digest, but of course there're no guarantees it will kick off straight away and do

84

well enough to pay for the space.'

In that second she knew what he wanted from her. What didn't click straight away was how he knew about her and Calvin and why he assumed they were a proper couple. She had no leverage over Calvin and didn't want it.

Then Shey realized. She glared at LB and the bastard couldn't even look at her. He was as spineless as a gummy bear, and as twisted as they come. To think she'd felt sorry for his marital problems. More. Fool. Her.

She turned back to Marco. 'You want me to ask Calvin to lower the rent.'

Marco nodded, smiling at her in a way that made her feel like a traitor. The reason she was here now made perfect sense. Blackmail, pure and simple. The walls had ears at *Storm* and no one other than Calvin knew she was meeting Marco tonight. There would be no proof for her if this all went the way she knew it would.

'And what if I say no?' Not really a question she needed to ask.

'Then you won't have a job. We've already hired another assistant for Jude, and if he can't work on the new feature, he'll return to page seven with his new assistant.'

Her mind spun. She could go to Calvin, let him apologize like he'd tried to do before she stormed out, persuade him to lower the rent and secure her dream job. Be like that bitch who had taken all his money.

Or she could hit the job sites and end up working for something cringe-worthy like the modern dog magazine. She revolted from the idea, but Marco wasn't giving her time to think. He strummed his fingers on the wooden table, scrutinizing her like a bug he could squish.

There wasn't any doubt about her answer. And she gave it to him without further hesitation.

# Chapter Nine

Calvin found himself at Shey's apartment by nine that evening. The guilt of his parting words to her made him restless and he was anxious to make things right with her, even if this was the end of their time together.

One of her roommates buzzed him in and opened the door when he got to it. 'Is she here?' he asked the blonde.

'I hope you're here to grovel.' The woman was tiny, but the fierceness in her expression cut him to bits.

Because he'd cut *Shey* to bits. 'I am.'

'Flowers wouldn't have broken the bank.'

He scrubbed a hand over his face. 'I think it will take more than flowers to make this up to her.'

The red-head let him in. He followed her through to a longue surrounded by vases of different kinds of fresh flowers, and was glad he hadn't brought any. A blonde glared at him from a leather sofa, then went back to reading a book she had open on her lap. He definitely deserved to feel this awful, and it warmed him to know Shey had friends who cared about her.

'Where is she?' he asked the red-head.

'In her room. She won't come out.' She pointed down the hall. 'Second door on the left.'

He took a step in the direction she'd pointed but she grabbed his arm. 'After everything she's sacrificed, you better be nice or Georgia and I will tie you down and cut off your balls with a rusty knife.'

Ah, she must be Eloisa, though from Shey's description of her friends he would have expected something like that from Georgia.

'Sacrifice?' he asked, but then didn't wait for an answer. Just like him, she'd given up her own rules to keep herself safe and he'd hurt her. 'Okay, rusty knife. Got it.'

Eloisa released him and he made his way to Shey's room. There was no answer when he knocked, so he opened the door. Shey was wrapped in a duvet facing the other side of the room, but her shoulders shook like she was crying. His heart ripped in two seeing her like that, and knowing he was the one to cause her pain.

'Shey, I'm so, so sorry about today.' He crossed the room, but didn't dare sit next to her. 'I didn't mean what I said. I was angry that you assumed I cheated on Jane. I never did. She had affairs, which I never found out about until she took every dime I had, but none of that excuses the way I treated you.'

She didn't turn. 'I don't care about that. Not anymore.'

Something shifted in his chest, stalling his heart and blocking his air supply. This couldn't be the end, they couldn't be over so quickly.

'I know I fucked up. I'm truly sorry, but I don't want this to be over.'

She turned to him, her eyes rimmed red, and Calvin had a horrible feeling that he wasn't the only cause of her pain. They'd only known each other for just over a week, though they'd spent a lot of time together. He'd grown closer to her than he had anyone, but one argument shouldn't have destroyed her. She was so much stronger than that.

'Shey, what happened with Marco?' He crouched by the side of the bed; had to work to keep his voice even. 'If he hurt you I'll—'

'There's nothing you can do.' Her voice was quiet, dead even. 'I don't work for *Storm* anymore. They fired me.'

His hands fisted on the sheets. 'Why?'

Shey turned back to face the wall, shrugging under the covers. 'Doesn't matter.'

Like hell it didn't. Calvin was going to pay Marco a visit. He wanted the twelfth floor? Well, he could work for it. Calvin had signed the contract but hadn't sent Marco his copy. It was easy enough to rip it up, which he would if that bastard didn't rehire her, or at least give her a glowing reference.

'I'll fix this,' he promised.

She sat up and turned to face him so fast he thought he might get whiplash. 'You'll leave it alone. There's nothing you can do and I don't want you to. What's the point, Calvin? You and I are a few nights away from never seeing each other again, and honestly I don't see a point in keeping this going.'

He gritted his teeth and fought the urge to reach for her, shake some sense into her. 'We don't need a time limit. This doesn't have to be over.'

Shit, just what he hadn't wanted to say, but panic made him desperate. Extending their time together would only make it harder to leave down the line.

'I suppose you want it all? Love, marriage and two point four children? Get real Calvin, we both know that won't happen and I don't want to fall for someone who'll drop me the second he gets bored.'

'You could never bore me.'

It was the best defense he had, because he couldn't deny the rest. Marriage, kids, any kind of future beyond what they had now wasn't what he wanted. And that wouldn't be fair to her, to live separately, to never have any kind of commitment from him other than his word that he wouldn't fuck anyone else. The scars Jane left ran deep, and though Shey was nothing like her, he couldn't risk this... *relationship* ending the same as his marriage. With him left with nothing.

It would be dangerous letting her into his heart, his life, and would cost him if they ever broke up. What he felt for Shey now far surpassed what he thought he felt for Jane. Letting Shey go would be more than him not being able to give her what she one day wanted. It was also self-preservation.

Her gaze softened. 'But we could never be what the other needs. I need security, now more than ever. And you need to be free, because you could never truly trust me. You'd always be wondering when I was going to walk out and leave you with nothing.'

She touched the side of his face and he caught her wrist, flattened her palm against his cheek and tried to breathe through the agony of knowing this was goodbye. 'I'll never forget you, gorgeous. Ever.'

Her eyes filled, and his vision got a little blurry too. To distract them both, he caught her face in his palms and kissed her too softly, too briefly. It didn't stop his whole body firing to life like it had been weeks and not hours since he made love to her.

Calvin pulled away. Rose from the floor. Couldn't take his eyes off her. Her expression crumpled and her amber eyes shone with the grief he felt.

He didn't have parting words, wasn't sure if he could speak. But he had a plan. He was going to make things right for her if it was the last thing he did, starting tomorrow with a visit to *Storm*.

\*\*\*

Shey was still shaking an hour after Calvin left.

Really left.

For the last time.

Her heart was broken, utterly shattered, and all that crap she'd spewed about not wanting to fall for him was the biggest lie she'd ever told. She'd fallen all right. Hard, and there was no going back from that.

But this was better now she could get over him. Move on. Look for work. A glance down at herself showed she was as much of a mess as everything else in her life.

Pulling herself together, she washed her puffy face and prepared for the inquisition. Georgia was reading on the sofa, while Eloisa was glued to America's Next Top Model, and look, mommy dearest was a guest on tonight's show, looking more put-together than freshly made dough.

'Will you guys help me send out my resume?' Shey asked.

Both turned her with shocked expressions. Shey never asked anyone for help, but she was on a mission to get her life back on track. The sooner the better. And the busier she was, the less time she had to pine over Calvin.

'I don't know what the hell he said in there, but I think I like him.' Since Georgia rarely liked anyone, that was saying something.

'He didn't say anything.'

Not even to fight for her, not even to reassure her she'd have more with him someday. And that was the motivation she needed to get her ass out of bed and get on with her life. Her mom had been right. She couldn't rely on a man, but unlike Felicity, she had friends. Friends who cared and were willing to help at the drop of a hat. And Shey loved them for it.

It was obvious from their mmhmm's they didn't believe her. But she ignored them and grabbed her laptop. 'First up, job-hunting.'

Eloisa switched off the box and picked up her own laptop, Georgia pulled out her iPad, and the three of them got to work.

***

Mandy didn't seem surprised to see Calvin when he arrived at *Storm*, though she'd probably heard about Shey by now. What did seem to surprise her was that Marco met him at the reception desk, instead of asking for her to show Calvin to his office.

Calvin was happy with the arrangement; it gave him more of an opportunity to show the bastard how furious he was and make

Marco sweat that little bit longer.

Marco led him through to his plush office suite, with a full wall made of glass looking out over New York. Calvin slid into a chair without being offered, and placed his briefcase holding the contract on his lap.

'Personally delivering the tenancy agreement?' Marco asked with a raised brow that said the fucker knew why Calvin was there.

'Let's cut the shit, shall we?'

Marco took the seat opposite him and nodded.

'Mind telling me why you fired Shey Lopez?'

The guy's eyebrows hit his hairline. 'She didn't tell you?'

Fuck, he should have opened with something that didn't show he knew zero. 'I'm asking for the reason *you* fired her, not why you told her you did.'

'If she told you anything at all, you wouldn't be asking me.' Marco smiled and Calvin wanted to wipe it off his face.

'I'm going to make this clear. If you want the twelfth floor, I'd suggest you reconsider her employment.' But if Shey didn't want to come back, what would be the point? 'Or recommend her to one of the other magazines in the city.'

'Shey was given a choice.' Marco's expression got serious. 'We're reorganizing staff, opening a new magazine, and that takes money. You drove a hard bargain. If I couldn't get a discount on the rent, the capital for the new venture would be too limited to go ahead.'

His stomach shifted. Calvin didn't like the sound of where the guy was going.

'Shey has been dating you, and I offered her the position of editor. For this to happen she had to convince you to lower the rent.'

Calvin's fists clenched. 'You blackmailed her?'

'I offered her a conditional promotion.'

Was this guy fucking insane? Then it hit him. Shey must have said no, knowing they would fire her if she didn't bow to the bastard's demands. She refused to ask that of him, even when losing her dream job was at stake.

It didn't make sense. Why the hell would she do that? Sure, they'd argued, but he had tried to apologize and she must know by now he'd do almost anything for her. He'd broken his own rules to make her happy. Twice, for Christ's sake.

'So you canned her when she said no.' His voice was cold with rage.

Marco shook his head. 'Her position was already taken by another, although for the new magazine. Even so, I did not fire her.'

'You backed her into a corner so she had no choice.' Calvin had to get out of here before he put the bastard through the glass wall.

'Shey told me to shove my job up my ass. Hardly the same as me firing her.'

Fury cracked Calvin wide open, until something else overpowered him. Shey had given up so much because she wouldn't ask him for anything. She knew how his marriage had given him trust issues, even when she didn't know all the details and refused to use him to get what she wanted.

For the first time since his father died, he felt like he could trust another person implicitly. And it wasn't just trust, but pure, unadulterated love that sang through his soul. He hadn't loved Jane really, and it wasn't until he met Shey he realized that. Somehow, knowing she'd destroy her own dreams instead of asking him to lower the rent, made him certain he could have a future with her.

He'd fucked things up with Shey, but he'd make that right if it was the last thing he did.

'If you don't get on your knees in front of her and grovel, I'll rip up the agreement. And if you dare try to sabotage her finding work anywhere else in this city, the second the lease is up on *Storm* you'll be out on your ass.'

Calvin didn't wait for Marco's compliance. The fucker liked his fancy office up there in the sky, and if he wanted to keep it he had to play on Calvin's terms.

As he left the building, a familiar woman stopped him in his tracks.

'Is Shey here?' Felicity asked.

Calvin was about to dismiss her, when it struck him. Today maybe he could right two wrongs against Shey. 'She doesn't work here anymore.'

Felicity's face, so similar to Shey's, dropped. Wringing her fingers in front of her, she pleaded with wide amber eyes. 'Can you tell me her address? I need to see her.'

'You don't know where your daughter lives?'

Her eyes narrowed. 'We haven't been close. I was hoping to change that.'

Calvin folded his arms. If the witch was going through a new I-need-a-daughter-fad, he wasn't letting her anywhere near Shey if he could help it. The woman had hurt her enough, and he owed Shey so much.

'What's changed?' he asked, the question laced with contempt.

Felicity put a hand on her hip. 'Are you going to tell me where she is?'

'Maybe, when I'm sure you're not going to treat her like the bane of your existence.'

Her eyes grew sad, and her shoulders slumped. 'I… things were tough when Shey was born.' Glancing around at the people rushing past, she murmured, 'Can we do this somewhere more private?'

Shaking his head, he glared at her. 'Always worried about what other people think. Tell me why the sudden turnaround and I'll decide whether to listen or leave right now.'

Calvin listened as she explained, wondering whether she was playing him or if she was serious. Deciding to give her the benefit of the doubt, he escorted her to a coffee house down the street so he could find out more. After all, if Felicity meant what she was saying, he had another idea to make everything up to Shey.

# Chapter Ten

Everything considered, the week was shaping up great. Shey tossed the keys on the breakfast bar and headed for the fridge. This early in the day, a celebratory orange juice was all that was reasonable though champagne wouldn't go amiss. Her first interview with an up-and-coming magazine had gone better than she'd hoped. Glamorous wasn't as high class as *Storm* but it was on its way with nationwide distribution and fantastic sales.

And the job they'd offered her at the end of the presentation had been more than she could get her head around. Creative Director. Her. And it was all thanks to LB for making it possible. Apparently Jude had gone out of his way to contact all the magazines in New York, recommending her to everyone who would listen. Maybe he did have a heart after all.

The urge to tell everyone she loved was strong, but Georgia and Eloisa were still at work. And Calvin... no, she wasn't going there. Keeping her mind off him had been harder than she'd thought and it still made her heart ache. Today was a day for celebrating not drowning in misery.

The phone rang and she darted into the sitting room, lifting the whole thing off the side table. She couldn't wait to tell the girls. 'Hello?'

'Shey? I'm glad I caught you.'

Ugh, Marco. She wasn't glad, not at all.

'I don't have anything to say to you.'

Well, that wasn't true, but what she wanted to say wasn't polite.

'I want to apologize for the way I treated you. It was callous, and I want you to come back. On a higher salary than before, obviously.'

Shey was about to tell him to shove it when a thought hit her. 'What changed your mind?'

He laughed, but it sounded more nervous than amused. 'Your boyfriend drives a hard bargain.'

Shocked speechless, she could only stare at her flabbergasted expression in the mirror on the wall. Calvin had done this, when she'd asked him to leave it alone? But there was the more pressing question of *why*. Was it guilt or something else driving him?

'Shey? Will you come back?' Marco asked impatiently.

'No Marco, I have another job. Thanks for your offer.' She hung up, not giving her old boss another thought.

Before she could chicken out Shey pulled out her cell, scrolled to Calvin's number, and hit call. Someone who wanted casual sex didn't care whether the person they were fucking, or no longer fucking, had a job. Especially since she'd been the one to end things between them. There was more going on, and she had to find out what or she'd drive herself mad.

'Shey? Is everything all right?' he answered.

Did she imagine the grit in his voice, the panic? 'Marco called. What did you do?'

'Can we meet? I don't want to do this over the phone.'

The fact he asked instead of demanded didn't sit right with her. Calvin never asked, not in a way that made 'no' an option anyway. 'Okay. I'm free tonight.'

Was that an exhale of relief?

'I'll pick you up at seven and take you to dinner.'

'Um… I'd rather not if you don't mind.' If she was going to break down when they said goodbye, she wanted to do it in private.

'Georgia and Eloisa won't be home until after six if you want to come here.'

There was a pause, and then, 'I'll be there soon, but Shey, don't make plans tonight. I need you to come somewhere with me.'

'Calvin—'

'I'll explain later, I'm on my way.'

The line cut off and she could only stare at the phone in her hand.

By the time the buzzer sounded, she was no closer to figuring out what he wanted from her. More sex was out of the question. She loved him too much and wouldn't survive the break-up. But the second she opened the door, saw him standing there in an immaculate suit, dark circles under his eyes and an unshaven jaw, she melted.

Agony burned in his eyes, like losing her had cost him so much. She never dreamed he had fallen too, even though they connected in every way. He took her face in his palms and looked down at her with longing, pride and… love?

Shey swallowed. It couldn't be love, and so what if it was? Didn't change anything, not really.

'Shey, I've missed you.' His lips brushed against her forehead, his stubble tickling her skin.

Fighting her yearning, she tried to call up anger at what he'd done. 'I told you not to visit Marco.'

His hands dropped from her face. 'You failed to mention he wanted you to make me lower the rent, or that you told him to shove his job.'

Was he pissed? His expression had hardened, but if anyone should be angry it was her. 'It was that or be fired.'

His eyes softened. 'I know. Shey, you should have come to me. I would have helped you.'

He reached for her, but must have thought better of it because he dropped his arm. She wanted him to touch her, hold her and tell her everything would work out fine. Was that so bad? But life had a balance. She'd scored a great job. It was way too much to ask that Calvin would do a one-eighty on his opinion of commitment.

She hugged herself. 'I didn't want to ask you to give up more money. I'm not Jane; I wouldn't take from you like that.'

'I know that too.' He came closer, the scent of him making her long for more than she could have. 'Though I didn't realize it until I'd spoken to Marco. I always had the fear that if I made another commitment it would backfire on me. Leave me with nothing other than huge debts.'

She nodded. The reason for his divorce still rested heavily on her chest. Her chin dipped, but of course he tipped it back up. Though his expression shadowed any emotion, he met her gaze with determination.

'I realize I've given you every reason to think the worst of me. I refused to talk openly about the dissolution of my marriage, and for that I'm truly sorry. What Jane did pretty much castrated me, and I never thought I could trust a woman after that.'

Her eyes stung with unshed tears. It was past time she knew, and asking the questions she needed to was the only way she'd find out. 'What happened?'

'We drifted apart, later I found out she had met someone else, but if she left on her own she'd have left with nothing.' Calvin squeezed his eyes shut and she cupped his stubble-covered jaw with her hands. 'She set up a honey trap for me, and I ended up drugged. Though I wasn't capable of doing more than being straddled by the woman, half-dressed, she managed to get enough incriminating evidence to prove an affair to the divorce courts. Jane walked away a wealthy woman.'

Shey gasped. Tears welled in her eyes then spilled over. 'Calvin—'

'Don't.' His finger cut off her words. 'I'm just trying to explain why it was hard for me to accept what we have. To trust you.'

'You know, there are ways to avoid that. Pre-nups, for instance.' Biting her tongue, she wished she'd kept her mouth shut.

But her comment didn't seem to faze him. He smiled. 'I don't need that with you.'

No, because there'd be no future with them, not after everything he'd been through. Her heart twisted.

Calvin's arms came around her, but she shoved him away. 'I can't—'

'Shey, did you hear what I said? I won't ask you for a pre-nup if we ever get married. I trust you, more than anyone.' His eyes scorched with honesty.

Her head felt fuzzy. 'What?'

Warm lips hit her jaw for a second and she shuddered.

'You're not Jane. I know that now.'

Her eyes widened. 'What are you talking about?'

'Us. Where we go from here.' He cupped her face with both hands. 'I love you, Shey. So much. The last week has been hell.'

Her eyes blurred, but she blinked the tears away. Buried what little hope she had. 'Why wait a week to tell me, Calvin? If I hadn't called—'

'I wanted tonight to be a surprise. Your roommates said you didn't have plans, so I've arranged dinner.'

She remembered he said with someone else and her suspicions grew. 'Who with?'

He sighed, and that lazy grin appeared but it didn't reach his eyes. 'I've just told you I love you and you're giving me a hard time?'

Shit, he was right. She was a class-A bitch. But if she admitted how she felt for him, there was no going back. She'd have to trust in him, believe that he'd always be there, and what if somewhere down the line he left? She'd end up like Felicity, clinging to her youth and cougaring around town with a twink.

'Stop thinking. What does your heart tell you?' he asked.

Shey did, and took the risk. 'That I love you.'

Calvin pulled her back into his arms, and she didn't fight him this time. She met his mouth with her own, hungry and desperate for him after time apart. He devoured her, making her dizzy and hot all over.

He broke the kiss too soon, gasping. 'If I take you to bed now, there's no coming out until tomorrow, and I want you to come with me tonight.'

She shook her head, trying to clear it. 'I don't get it. Are you saying you've changed your mind, that one day you might want to marry me, after everything she put you through?'

It was hard to believe that cow could do what she did to Calvin. He was the best man she'd known. The woman must be clinically insane.

Calvin nuzzled his nose against her jaw. 'I know your career is important to you, and that's your main focus now. I can't promise you what the future will hold, but I love you so much I'm willing to risk anything for us to have a chance, are you?'

Was she? Shey didn't know. He wasn't offering her much other than a real relationship; who knew where they'd go or how long they would last?

He planted a kiss on the tip of her nose. 'The wait's killing me.'

She could see that in his eyes. All this was new to him. He'd clearly sworn off any kind of commitment and what he was offering her was much more than she ever thought he could. What had she given him?

'You come first, Calvin. Not my career. I thought I'd proved that to you.'

'You have, and I can't tell you how much it means to me.'

He didn't have to. It was there in the way he looked at her like she was the best thing that had ever happened to him.

'I got a new job as a creative editor with *Glamorous*.' She couldn't hold back the excitement finally getting to tell him, and wasn't sure she could accept what he was offering, even though the thought of never seeing him again gave her chills. 'Things are starting to look up.'

'I hope they keep getting better.'

Shey didn't miss the apprehension in his eyes, which only sparked her worry. 'Second thoughts?'

'About you? Never.' Calvin shook his head as if to drive home the point. 'I invited Felicity to dinner.'

Shey had to replay the words in her head. 'You... *what*?'

'Give her a chance, Shey.'

'A chance? The woman doesn't even want me as a daughter.'

'She feels awful about that night at the restaurant, and she does want you, more than you know.' He frowned at her, like *she* was the unreasonable one.

'She must have done a number on you. I thought you couldn't stand her.' And there they were, ten minutes into hashing out their new relationship and they were arguing.

'She wants to make amends, Shey. Won't you be happier with your mother in your life?'

Shey shook her head, but not in answer to his question. 'Calvin, we're never going to work. Look at us, we're fighting already. This going behind my back is too much. I—'

He cursed. 'We'll fight, everyone does, but we can work this out.' He pulled her close. 'All I want is you in my life; you're all I've been able to think about since I met you. The idea of never seeing you again because you're too scared to take a risk on us terrifies me.'

Shey scowled at him. 'I'm not too scared.'

He cocked a brow, and she had to wonder if he wasn't right. She wasn't scared of him, per se. More that she'd invest herself in something she couldn't control the outcome of. But hadn't he proven to her time and time again that giving herself up to him completely was better than anything she'd ever experienced?

And Calvin was doing the same, putting his heart on the line when it had been stomped on by that ex-bitch's designer shoes, shoes that he no doubt paid for.

'Okay, I'm terrified,' she admitted. 'But I'm willing to take the risk on one condition.'

His brows drew together. 'Go on.'

'If I ask you not to do something—'

He pressed a finger to her lips and smiled. 'I bumped into Felicity after I saw Marco, I didn't go behind your back and technically you didn't ask me not to speak to her.'

'And?' Shey mumbled against his finger.

'I couldn't help giving her a piece of my mind for the way she treated you.'

He pulled her closer, and she let him. After all, she didn't want to fight with him for trying to help. How many guys would see that Felicity hurt her? None had, or cared. Calvin didn't just see her pain, he was trying to take it away. Trying to make her life complete.

'I don't think she realized how much she upset you, and I think she wants to start fresh. Her best friend just lost her daughter in a car accident. I don't think she realized what she had with you until it was taken away from someone close to her.' He tucked her hair behind her ears. 'I'll be with you. I won't let her hurt you again—though I don't think she will. You're everything to me, Shey.'

Blinking, she tried to figure out what angle her mother was playing, but there was a part of her that wondered, what if she wasn't? Of course she loved her mother, but life with her hadn't been easy.

Calvin used his thumb to smooth the line in her forehead and she relaxed the muscles beneath.

'I want you to be happy, and I know for all you can't stand your mother, you love her too. I'm sorry if I crossed a line.'

Shey brushed her lips against his. 'You didn't. Thank you, for everything. I promise to try to stop picking fights with you, but if I go too far, you'll need to pull me back.'

'I won't let it get out of hand.' His expression was deadpan serious.

'Oh, and how are you going to manage that?'

His lips quirked. 'Nothing a good spanking won't fix.'

She laughed for the first time in a week, and felt truly free. She had her man, a great job, and maybe even her mother if everything went well. There really was nothing Calvin wouldn't do for her.

'Well, Mr. Jones, maybe I like being spanked, ever thought about that?'

Calvin growled. 'Then I'll have to punish you by withholding my talents for a week.'

She pressed against him, feeling his erection hard against her stomach. 'I bet you'd cave in a day.'

'I'd put money on it,' he said, then kissed her too briefly. 'We're really going to give this a shot?'

Shey beamed at him. With no more doubts or hesitation, she said, 'You're worth the risk.'